VAN BURE[N]
DECATU[R]
W9-BUS-747

DISCARDED

ADVERTISING MURDER

ADVERTISING MURDER

•

Robert Scott

AVALON BOOKS
NEW YORK

5co

© Copyright 2007 by Robert Scott
All rights reserved.
All the characters in the book are fictitious,
and any resemblance to actual persons,
living or dead, is purely coincidental.
Published by Thomas Bouregy & Co., Inc.
160 Madison Avenue, New York, NY 10016

Library of Congress Cataloging-in-Publication Data
Scott, Robert, 1947–
Advertising murder / Robert Scott.
p. cm.
ISBN-13: 978-0-8034-9828-0 (hardcover : acid-free paper)
1. Ex-police officers—Fiction. I. Title.
PS3619.C6835A38 2007
813'.6—dc22
2006101693

PRINTED IN THE UNITED STATES OF AMERICA
ON ACID-FREE PAPER
BY HADDON CRAFTSMEN, BLOOMSBURG, PENNSYLVANIA

⁹/₀₇
Kausegy

To Shirley, who never stopped believing.
Thanks. You're the best.

Prologue

*Men loved darkness rather than light,
because their deeds were evil.*
(John 3:19, The Bible, King James Version)

Two shadows faced each other in the subdued lighting. It was night.

One had come to this place expecting that, with luck, life might be changed and hope might be granted. The other aspired to settle a difference of opinion; to right a perceived wrong; to put an end to things, once and for all. Their discussion had been heated.

"What is your decision?" The voice was angry and betrayed a deep frustration.

"I can't—I won't do what you ask. It goes against everything I have come to believe in. It's completely unreasonable." Determination in the tone gave notice that the discussion should come to an end.

"You must do what I ask."

"I will not. And you can't force me."

1

"But you must." Anger rose and rage filled the speaker's heart and countenance.

The argument continued back and forth with no sign or resolution. Voices were raised in anger, unheard by others. A hand was raised. The light reflected off a shining surface.

One problem was solved. Another created.

Chapter One

Jack Elton drove up the hill, past the bus terminal. Heading back home, after an evening of partying with his friends, he slumped in the driver's seat and wished he could afford a better car—at least one with a heater that worked. He swiped at the window with the back of his hand but only managed to clear away some of the condensation. The glass was smeared so that he was no better off than before.

The rain of the previous evening had left the streets wet and reflecting the neon and halogen of the lights on the main street. It was early morning and the city wasn't yet fully awake. Taxi drivers, waiting for a call or a fare, napped in their cars, parked along the curb. A few hardy street people huddled against the doorways of buildings.

Had the night out been worth the pain? Jack knew that his head was going to hurt in a few more hours. Why did he do such foolish things? It was bad enough that he had drunk too much, but it bothered him that he had engaged in sophomoric drinking games with his buddies that caused him to imbibe without even the time to savor the alcohol.

3

He had not won at beer guzzling, but had only missed reaching that lofty goal by half a pint. It was extremely small consolation that the winner would have a headache of approximately the same size as Jack's after the bragging was over.

He had enjoyed the companionship of his friends, both male and female, at the impromptu gathering. Folks talked about their lives in a manner intended to impress. After a little drinking, it was easy to be bold. A few more drinks and folks began to believe their own lies. A little more alcohol and no one gave a damn about what was being said. Everybody was your 'good buddy' and the appellation was said with a slur in the speech.

He had watched with faintly concealed amusement as Dick, an office clerk in an obscure real estate office on the outskirts of town, tried to convince a clearly uninterested young thing that he was the president of the company.

She tried to look as if she was listening while Dick went on and on about his high position and heavy responsibility. She had long legs and a short skirt and didn't seem to care much about the relative position of either. The eyes of the pseudo-executive moved back and forth between her chest and her thighs. It wouldn't matter whether she was listening or not. Jack had enough of his wits about him to know that, no matter what, he never wanted to be the type of man Dick was.

None of the girls appealed to Jack. Though the oncoming effects of the alcohol had an arousing effect on his libido and masked even the imperfections of the truly unattractive ones, he could not bring himself to make any advances to the female partiers.

It was a lonely drive and Jack had hoped that he would be a little luckier in love. His wishing had not made it so. He had a vision in his mind—a beautiful face he had seen before. It had been a one-time encounter and then she had faded away. Jack wished he had been paying more attention to details that night. She wasn't part of the group he had encountered this evening. He was convinced she was higher class than that. Probably too high for him.

He hated going home alone, especially in the early morning. The room would be cold. He would be completely alone. Life was unexciting.

He watched a street-sweeper wetting down the already damp road and wondered at the waste.

A short man picked up a sandwich board from the sidewalk and walked it about in a sort of halting dance, as if unsure what to do with it. The clock on the tourist information building read 5:37 A.M.

Jack's day was going to be a busy one. But right now, he didn't know that. His plan, at the moment, included going to bed and sleeping off some of the alcoholic buzz that was short-circuiting much of his thought processes. The sound of his car's engine echoed in his brain and made him wince.

He spotted a police cruiser and slowed down. No use giving them a reason to stop him.

Jack thought back to the days when law enforcement had been his job. Had it not been for a back injury, and some unfortunate encounters with less-than-law-abiding folks, who pretty much destroyed his reputation and career, he might not have to earn his living as a process server and part-time investigator. There wasn't much call for that sort of thing in a city where the police department was efficient and the crime rate was relatively low. But Jack could not get law enforcement, and the excitement of the quest for justice, out of his blood.

At one time, he had been one of the best cops in the city.

He waved at the officers through his misted window. They

didn't wave back. He was a nobody now. His time in the spotlight was over. He felt more than the physical pain of his misadventure, even though it had been six years since it all happened.

Jack turned off the road to the west, and crossed the bridge that would take him back to his home, on the other side of the waterway.

It would soon be dawn. He needed to get inside. If the sun rose while he was outside, his day would be ruined.

It wasn't that he was afraid he would turn into something supernatural. It there was one thing Jack Elton was not, it was superstitious. He'd broken mirrors without fear of bad luck, walked in one door of a house and out the other without feeling he had to be on the look-out for the grim reaper. He's even been known to spill salt and not to throw any over his shoulder. It was just a waste of good salt, in his way of thinking.

The real problem was that his body clock would not let him sleep if he carried the image of the dawning of the day into his cramped little apartment, upstairs from his office, over the thrift store that looked out on the two-lane road.

As he rounded the corner, a half block from home, Jack checked to see that the road was clear then made a U-turn that brought him to the edge of the sidewalk in front of his building. He was now facing back into town.

He checked the car windows all around, closed the one on the driver's side that he had cracked open in hopes of clearing the windshield, and leaned his weight against the door. It resisted briefly before opening with a metallic squeak. He made a mental note—again—to bring out the can of WD-40, for the locks and hinges, the next time he left the office.

If mental notes were written on Post-Its, he'd never be

able to see where he was going. Some of his reminders were so old that the sticky stuff had worn off and they kept on getting lost in the other activities he was involved in. He had no idea how many of the WD-40 Post-Its were up there, in his brain, but there had been quite a few, and they had all been ignored.

The sky had begun to lighten as he fumbled for his keys. A purple glow was rising in the east. The sun would not be far behind. The weather had begun to cool as Fall set in, and his fingers weren't working too well in the early-morning cold and damp. Jack made a mental note to look for his gloves. He finally found the right key, and let himself in. He ascended to the third floor, pulling himself up the banister with his right hand. As he rounded the landing on the second floor, he looked toward his office to make sure all the lights were out and the 'Sorry, We're Closed' sign was still hanging on the knob. He wouldn't be sorry about being closed today, he thought.

On the third floor he entered his apartment and threw his coat over a chair. Without undressing, he lay down on the bed and was soon snoring.

The city awakens early when there is work to be done. The highway begins to fill with vehicles at about six, and those with business in downtown continue to flow in waves until nine, the absolute latest that a respectable enterprise can post as the beginning of its daily endeavors

By bus, car, and bicycle, they come. There is no train anymore but some folks continue to hope that rail travel will revive and ease the morning gridlock. They come in the uniform of their business unless, of course, they have chosen to use two-wheeled transport. The bicycle lanes are full of colorful, and eclectic, riding gear. Not all are careful how they use the road. Many motorists marvel that more of them don't become rainbow road kill. A lot of cyclists, watching the car drivers, are afraid too.

The parade of commuters moves slowly into the city core five days a week.

The rising sun sent its rays into the windows of the high-rise buildings in the center of the city. In the eleventh-floor offices of Biggs, Wilberforce, Hutton, and Small, a bright beam slowly traced across the room, illuminating work stations, desks, the green carpet, and the body of a woman surrounded by an impressive pool of drying blood. The digital clock across from the reception desk read 7:59 A.M. In less than one minute, the day would have a completely different start than anyone could have imagined.

Abba deBie came briskly to the office door, as she did every day at that time. Clutching a bundle of file folders to her chest, she searched in her coat pocket. She pulled out her hand and squinted at the key ring, selecting the one with the red plastic cover on the end. Abba had learned, before now, that when you are in a hurry, it is frustrating to have to try a whole series of similar keys before you can get in. She leaned on the door for support, and was surprised to discover that it opened.

How did that get left unlocked? Someone is going to be in deep trouble, she thought.

When you enter the Biggs, Wilberforce, Hutton, and Small office, a reception counter prevents a clear view of the area. This, of course, is intentional. Customers coming and going to the advertising firm do not need to see the activities, or absence thereof, of the folks who ordinarily occupy the desks.

Abba placed the files on the counter, and slipped off her coat. She hung it on the rack behind the counter, walked around to the work area, and was immediately confronted by what had once been the life blood of whoever had taken up occupancy of a portion of the floor. Her scream of alarm gave notice of the discovery up and down the hall.

Abba's horror attracted a lot more attention as people began to arrive at the office for work. They found her wringing her hands and pacing back and forth, staring out the window that overlooked the main street. It was evident she was in no shape to summon help. One of the secretaries had snatched up a phone as soon as she realized the situation. Nine–one–one had been called and the police were on their way.

There were sirens in the distance, but no one could be sure that they were the ones intended for the office building. In a large city, there are many occasions for the police, fire and rescue, or an ambulance crew, to want to clear the way to one place or another. Morning traffic was clogging the arteries into the city, and not everyone pulled over to one side at the sound of emergency vehicles.

Chapter Two

Jess Grinnell was the office manager. She was a round woman who had served the company for many years.

Jess always gave the appearance of efficiency. A student of the old school of office administration, she always arrived in an impeccable business attire—gray skirt; white blouse, often with a ruffle at the neck; matching gray jacket; and her gray hair perfectly coiffed and sprayed so that it looked almost bulletproof.

The other women looked to Jess as the 'mother hen.' She took good care of her staff and was especially close to the younger ones whom she felt needed someone they could turn to for advice and assistance.

This morning, her counseling abilities were being sorely tried. Every time someone new entered the office, she needed to give another explanation and more traffic direction. The scene had been one of pure chaos as, one by one, staff had entered the area and encountered the sight which had greeted Abba only a little earlier.

Someone—actually, one of the younger copywriters—

had found a blanket in an office cupboard and, without thinking about the consequences of his actions, had draped the dead body to protect it from prying eyes.

Steven Chalmers had not realized that, in the process of protecting the poor woman from the inquisitive stares of his fellow employees, he might have disturbed vital evidence. While his gesture was surely appreciated by the others, it was going to cause some problems for the police, with their limited forensic capabilities.

People stood around the perimeter of the room in little groups unsure of what to do. Lacking further direction, they engaged in whispered, though animated, conversations. The body in the office had a chilling effect on their interaction. From time to time someone would look toward the mound on the floor and turn back to their group in silence.

The voice on the other end of the nine-one-one call had said that everyone should stay for interrogation by the investigating officers. The operator had neglected to mention that folks who arrived later didn't need to be there. She made no mention of the fact that the crime scene would be closed for business. Her job was just to get the facts of the matter and dispatch the appropriate individuals.

No one was monitoring the door. The office was becoming crowded.

That all changed with the arrival of the police, who quickly took charge of the crime scene. One of the constables checked for a pulse but found no signs of life. Soon the office had been taped off, the supervisor of the watch informed, and more help had been summoned to keep new arrivals from disturbing what little evidence might have been left.

"Are you going to be okay?" Jess looked at Abba with tired, inquiring eyes.

"Oh, this is most upsetting. This is a terrible tragedy. I am beside myself with upset."

Abba had a tendency to lapse into the characteristic speech pattern of someone new to the English language when she was excited, or frightened. It was clear that this had come as a terrible shock to her system.

Her dark face was, nevertheless, flushed. Her eyes darted back and forth, as if expecting the specter of another dead body to materialize. She was perspiring heavily.

Jess escorted the young woman to an empty cubicle and convinced her to sit down. Abba's right leg shook visibly, and she covered her face with her hands. Her eyes were red from crying. Her constantly running her hands through her long jet-black hair accentuated the look of agitation.

Two uniformed police officers had arrived shortly after the call. They had begun a preliminary inquiry but it was plain that this was going to be a matter for the detectives. They radioed to headquarters with the news that they truly had a murder to deal with.

The office clock showed 8:42 A.M. when two officers from the homicide division presented themselves at the reception desk. Whether because of limited manpower, slow moving traffic, or some other reason, it had taken almost a half hour for them to arrive.

"I'm Chief Detective Brown, and this here's Detective Willis. Who's in charge here?"

"Ordinarily, our boss would be able to help you, officers, but he is not in until nine, or a little later, on Thursday mornings. Mrs. Grinnell can help you, I think."

Apparently no one had thought to call the man whose job was to oversee everything that happened at the offices of Biggs, Wilberforce, Hutton, and Small. The detective looked put out by this revelation. His partner was writing furiously in a notebook he had produced from the inside pocket of his wrinkled brown suit jacket.

Debbie Agee, a pert blond with a good complexion and pleasing demeanor was everyone's choice for receptionist of the century. She escorted the two men around the counter and indicated Jess' head and shoulders over the top of the divider that separated the cubicle from the rest of the office.

Detective Willis moved to the body, pulled back the blanket, gave the face a cursory glance, and replaced the cover. He caught up with his superior by the entrance to Jess and Abba's sanctuary.

"Crime scene's been compromised," the younger man said, not too quietly, to the senior officer.

The chief detective went through the introductions again and asked for details.

"I know this is hard for you, miss, but I need you to be as clear as possible about what you saw when you came in this morning. Now, before you start, did anyone touch anything around the body?"

Abba's sad eyes turned briefly to the face of the officer, and then she looked away.

"I arrived at my regular time. I was carrying some files that I had been looking over last night. I left them on the counter. When I went to open the door, I found that it was already unlocked. This is a most peculiar state of affairs."

She was slipping into old speech habits again, as the thought of what she had discovered caused her further anguish.

"Go on," the senior officer said.

"As I said, I put the files on the counter and came back here. I have a desk over there, by the window." She pointed. "When I came into this part of the office, I found . . . I found . . ."

"The body." Detective Willis finished the sentence for her.

Brown gave him a look of disdain and turned back to Abba with an "and then what" raising of the eyebrows.

"Well, then, I'm afraid, I just sort of fell apart. I never expected to find anyone dead in the office. That's all I know. And no, I haven't touched anything—at least not intentionally. I almost tripped over her when I came in, but when I realized what it was, I stayed as far away as possible.

"As far as I know, no one has gotten too near to her, except Steve, when he got the blanket. People have been arriving for work and just walking in to find this." She waved her hand in the general direction of the body on the carpet.

"And who is, or was, the decedent—the, um, woman?" the chief detective asked. "Does anyone know?"

Abba began shaking her head.

Brown had spoken the question into the air and with enough volume that the folks around the office perimeter could hear. Almost as one, there was the shaking of heads and the muttering of "no" and ". . . haven't a clue."

Brown raised his eyebrows and looked at Jess Grinnell.

Detective Willis continued to write, a look of disgust on his face. It was plain that he did not have a lot of respect for the folks in this office, and he had no desire to hide the fact.

"I'm sorry, Officer, I have never seen this person before," Jess said. "As you may have gathered, she was not employed here."

"Have you any explanation for the open door? Does anyone know anything about it?"

"Miss deBie hasn't any idea how that could have happened. No one else knows how the door could have been unlocked either." Jess answered for Abba, who had begun crying again.

She continued, "Mr. Biggs was the last one out last night,

I believe. He said he was meeting with a client a little later in the evening and still had some paperwork to complete. He should be in within the hour. You might want to check with him."

"Be assured, ma'am, we will check with everyone before we are done. Maybe it would be best if someone called him in right now."

The younger detective, Willis, was asserting himself again.

"Keegan, be a good man and see what you can do about moving some of these folks out into the hallway. I've got a little more business with these ladies, and then you and I have more work to do."

Brown was trying to keep his partner from saying or doing anything else to make a bad situation worse.

The younger officer looked disappointed but quickly warmed to the new task of herding staff.

"Okay, now. Listen up folks. This here is a crime scene. We don't want to disturb the evidence any more than it already has been. You'll have to deal with me if you don't do as I say and do it quickly."

Willis was strutting about, making gestures to indicate the men and women should stay close to the walls, and move in single file.

After the office doors finally closed, and most of the previous audience was gone, Brown could still hear Keegan Willis, out in the hall, giving stern warnings and instructing complete obedience to the uniformed officers who had apparently just arrived to assist the others.

The chief detective needed to organize the interrogation of witnesses, if there were any. With it appearing as though the crime had been committed the previous evening, or earlier in the morning. It would be a grim task to try to track down the perpetrator unless, by some stroke of luck, that individual had not managed to get too far.

A team of specialists would be going from office to office, asking for any information that might help in solving the mystery that had appeared in the middle of the eleventh floor.

If there were any surveillance tapes, they would be checked for suspicious activity.

Brown shuddered to think of the time that would have to be spent checking out the owners of vehicles that were parked in the vicinity within the hours since the murder was committed. It had to be done. Maybe the fact that things happened during the night and early morning would work in his department's favor. There would have been fewer vehicles on the street, and in the parking lot, than there were now that the work day was in full swing.

What irked Brown was that he could not be sure exactly when the young woman died until the coroner had done his preliminary examination. The good doctor was out on the highway somewhere, dealing with the results of someone's road rage, or inattentiveness at the wheel. The golden forty-eight hours, during which most investigations either succeed or fail, were slipping away. He hoped that it wasn't too late.

The arrival of the paramedics was accompanied by the metallic clanking of a gurney and the sighing of the glass double door to the offices. They entered and proceeded to the blanket and the stain on the floor.

"You can check it out, if you want, but I'm quite sure we are too late for that one," Brown said, as he approached the man and woman in the blue jump suits.

One of the EMTs stooped and pulled back the blanket. He felt for a pulse and replaced the cloth, shaking his head.

The younger officer had just come in from his lecture in the hall.

"You can take her away once the coroner arrives and you've done the paperwork. He's tied up and can't come right away. Get a record of injuries and anything else you notice. I think the stab wounds to the chest and neck had something to do with her present state," he said.

Keegan Willis was as blunt as a butter knife and didn't always think before speaking. The uniformed officers looked in his direction with disdain, as he gave his less-than-professional opinion of the scene before them.

"I think we'd better leave well-enough alone for now," one of the paramedics said. "Best to let the coroner do his assessment before we even think of touching the body. Too bad the scene hasn't been kept undisturbed. Who put the blanket down?"

No one answered the question.

Though the city was relatively large, it was not financially able to afford its own Medical Examiner. It had to depend on the services of a Provincial Coroner who was stretched to the breaking point by the volume of auto accidents, unexplained sudden deaths, and the occasional bloody murder.

The officers busied themselves with getting a list of the names and addresses of the folks who had been in the office, and then suggested they all head home for the day. The coroner was at least two hours away at a multi-vehicle accident and, unfortunately, the scene in the office would not change for awhile.

The IDENT people still had their work to complete. There were photographs to be taken and measurements to be made. Trace evidence would be lifted, and anything out of the ordinary would need to be separated from the leavings of the day-to-day activities, and the unfortunate introduction of other elements, as a result of their inability to secure the scene before others arrived.

It was also highly likely that, when the investigation was over, someone might want to have the carpet cleaned. Today there would not be a lot of advertising business transacted by Biggs, Wilberforce, Hutton, and Small.

Chapter Three

Jack Elton had decided that today he would rest. There were no summonses to serve. His calendar was clear. He had an immense hangover. It gave him no consolation whatsoever that he had been able to predict the results of the previous evening's indiscretions.

Jack wasn't a particularly religious man but he thanked God that he had been able to find black-out curtains for his windows. When they were drawn, he couldn't tell the difference between day and night. He had made a habit of turning his clock radio so he couldn't see the time on those occasions when it seemed likely that an extended period of recuperation was called for. But then, the best laid plans can always be screwed up by a telephone that has not had the ringer turned off. And Jack's apartment didn't have an answering machine.

It was almost eleven when the phone began to call to him through the fog of sleep. He rolled over, wishing it into silence. Most folks gave up after five or six unanswered rings, but this morning, whoever was calling was persistent. Jack rolled to his left, felt for the receiver, and knocked it, clattering, to the floor.

He fished the handpiece up hand-over-hand and placed it to his ear.

"Speak," he said into the mouthpiece.

"Jack, it's Brendan. Look, I'm in a bit of trouble here and I think I could use your help. I need to see you at my office. Right away!"

"Uh, look Brendan, I'm kind of tied up today. Could we deal with this some other . . . ?"

"Jack, I wouldn't ordinarily do this, but I'm begging you to get over here as soon as you can. I can't talk on the phone but I can tell you that it's a matter of life and death. I've got to have someone to help me. I know you're still at home because this isn't your office number."

The voice sounded desperate.

"Brendan, I'd love to help. Really I would, but . . ."

"I'll be here waiting for you," said the voice at the other end of the line.

The phone went dead.

Jack lay in the darkness wondering why his old friend might need him in such a hurry. He reached out, fumbled for the clock, and turned it to face the bed. Ten fifty-three. He'd had almost five hours of sleep.

No rest for the wicked, he thought as he groped for the light switch. *This had better be important or I'll cause some serious noise in Brendan's quiet little world.*

He took as much time as he dared getting out of bed. He was already dressed in the clothes of the previous evening and made a stop in the bathroom. He ran his hand quickly through his mussed hair. He remembered to flush.

He made sure his apartment was locked and detoured briefly to his office on the second floor. There were no messages on the answering machine, and the only mail was bills, flyers, and the joyful news that he had been approved for yet another credit card.

As he locked the office and headed down into the street, he tried to reconcile the overdue bills with the breathless announcements of his good credit from people who wanted him to use their particular brand of plastic. He knew what he'd like to do to the writers of these epistles, but most of his ideas were illegal.

It was no wonder folks built up incredible debt loads by not paying attention to how they were using their cards. Spreading it out over a number of accounts would probably isolate someone from the pain of how much they actually owed. He had given up hurting himself like that long ago.

He needed coffee. For now it would have to wait. Maybe the pot would be on at Brendan's office.

Jack folded himself into his old car and, as always, gave a brief thought to how nice it would be to have a new model with more head and leg room.

Maybe some day. Maybe not.

He turned the key. The motor protested briefly and then, reluctantly, came to life. He pulled out into the mid-morning traffic and headed back to town.

Brendan needed him. Jack knew he had to help in whatever way he could.

His old friend was still happily married, as far as he knew. He was a partner in a successful business. Brendan had enough money, so he wouldn't need to steal. Speeding tickets didn't give rise to the sort of anxiety Brendan had displayed during the phone conversation. Jack couldn't think of a single thing that his buddy could have done to get himself in trouble. He'd said it was "life and death" though, hadn't he?

* * *

Brendan's place of business wasn't the tallest, but the building dominated the block. It housed a bank on the ground level.

At this hour, a lot of money appeared to be changing hands. The ATMs had lineups and, through the window, Jack could see that the tellers were being kept busy behind their counters. A long line of customers waited between the velvet ropes for the privilege of boosting the bottom line of one of the country's major financial institutions.

This, however, was not sufficient to distract Jack's attention from what appeared to be an indication that something was terribly wrong.

A couple of city police cars were almost parked outside the main entrance, their red, yellow, and blue flashers alternating. They had come to rest at various angles to the sidewalk, with no apparent concern for the flow of traffic.

An ambulance, with the back door open, was awaiting an occupant.

A separate lobby allowed access to offices on the floors above. An officer stood in the foyer, inside the double doors, indicating that interlopers were not welcome to use the elevators. Today, Jack could tell from the cop's demeanor, everyone was an intruder.

The officer wore a long-sleeved khaki shirt and a Kevlar vest. His arms were folded across his abdomen. His swollen belly strained at the various fasteners, and the belt of his navy trousers was slung well south of his middle.

Jack walked to the door, and flashed a smile.

"Morning, Dave. I've been asked to come here by Brendan Biggs. Can you let me in?"

Jack and Dave Simpson had once served together on the force until injury and innuendo had ended Officer Elton's career. In the past, they would have shared this experience as partners. Now, a wall separated them.

"I'm supposed to keep everyone away, Jack. Biggs' office is a crime scene right now. I don't have you on the list to go up."

He held a clipboard with a sheet of paper attached that Jack could not read.

"What sort of crime are we talking about here, Dave? Someone been stealing pencils from the boss' office?"

"I'm not at liberty to say, sir."

"Oops! Formal police talk. It's that bad, eh?"

"'Fraid so. Can't let anyone in who isn't on official business."

"I think I'm supposed to be here on 'official business.' " Jack raised both hands to eye level and made quotation marks by wiggling his fingers. "Okay if I call upstairs and get permission? Let me borrow your phone. Whaddaya say?"

"Jack, if you can get Detective Brown to let you in, you can be my guest." He unclipped his cell phone and handed it to his former partner.

"Aw, Dave, why didn't you tell me old Ted was up there? Piece of cake. Wait here."

"As if I'd go anywhere," the officer muttered, with a shrug of his shoulders and a shake of his head. He let the door close as Jack flipped the phone open.

Jack had a holy hatred of cell phones. At least, he disliked them enough not to want one of his own.

His response to friends, or folks in the mall who wanted him to buy one was, "People are always calling and disturbing you in the middle of things. I don't have much use for them—the phones, I mean."

He prepared to disturb Detective Brown, who was, apparently, right in the middle of something.

Jack dialed a number and spoke animatedly to whoever was on the other end. A smile flickered on his lips as he turned again to the front doors of the office building.

"Hang on, Ted. I'll pass you over to Officer Simpson. Just let him know it's okay."

Then, thrusting the phone toward the officer, who was holding one door ajar, "Here ya go, Dave. You're off the hook for this one."

The officer listened briefly, nodding at what he heard, and gave indication that the message had been received and understood. He folded the phone and clipped it to his belt again.

"If he says it's okay, who am I to stand in your way. Eleventh floor. I believe you know your way."

He made a sweeping gesture, with his arm, toward the bank of elevators in the center of the lobby.

"Thanks."

Jack headed across the polished marble floor. He pressed the 'up' button and waited. The soft sound of a bell heralded the coach's arrival. Steel doors opened with a rumble and he stepped in. He pressed the key for the eleventh floor. Seconds later he found himself in the middle of a scene of chaos.

A crowd milled about in the hallway in front of the office. The EMTs were still waiting for the coroner to arrive and let them be about their business. The curious from other floors persisted in taking a detour to gape into the office on their way to or from work. They left, chastised by the cops, and were disappointed that there was nothing to see from the hallway.

A uniformed officer, with a badge and a stern expression, protected the doorway, and let Jack through only after the okay had crackled into his walkie-talkie.

Jack shrugged past the half-open door, and its guardian, and rounded the edge of the counter. As he did, he noticed the young East Indian girl, sitting with an older woman, on the couch in the waiting area. The younger woman was obviously in a great deal of distress. A box of tissues sat on the table beside her. A wastebasket was half-full of wadded paper hankies. A fresh pot of coffee sat on the hot-plate beside them.

Jack helped himself to a paper cup and filled it. He hated the 'powdered cow' they used in the office but it was all they had. It would have to do for now.

He stirred the coffee absentmindedly and nodded to the two women who talked in hushed tones. The younger woman plucked another tissue and dabbed her eyes.

Abba had not calmed appreciably and startled visibly every time a phone rang or a walkie-talkie crackled.

Jack saw Detective Brown and his sidekick standing guard over the body. Brown, tall and thin, in a tailored business suit, massaged his chin with his left hand, looking every bit the professional crime fighter.

His companion wore no jacket. His hair seemed to go in every direction. The sleeves of his wrinkled blue shirt were damp with perspiration at the armpits. Keegan Willis needed a shave.

Every now and then, one of them would stoop and examine the body. They scribbled notes, and one would turn to the other, to make an observation. As Jack approached, both men fell silent.

"What have we got here?"

Jack looked to Brown as the authority.

"Dead body," said Willis with a smirk, arms folded across his chest.

Jack ignored him and waited for the chief detective to reply.

"Well Jack, the decedent here is a young female. Identity unknown. Early twenties. Some Asian, or Middle Eastern, blood. Difficult to tell right yet. She's been stabbed a number of times. Was found just before opening this morning."

Police talk. Jack felt like one of the team again. Brown was letting him into his world. It felt good to be back, even if only for a moment.

"She knew her attacker, then," Jack observed.

"Stabbings are personal, Jack. I think we can be fairly certain that she was at least acquainted with her attacker. Haven't found the weapon yet."

"But we will," said Willis, playing 'tough cop.'

"I'm sure you will. I'll let you get back to it, then."

"Why you here, Jack?" Brown asked.

"Biggs called. He's a friend. Said he had some trouble needed dealing with. I guess I can figure out what it is."

"You know Biggs? You don't know the half of it. Your friend has got himself into one deep pile of . . . trouble. By the looks of things, he's the prime suspect." Keegan Willis looked pleased with himself, as if he had just solved the crime.

Chapter Four

On the highway northwest of the city, the coroner's SUV was parked off the road, across from the entrance to the provincial park.

The services of the good doctor were necessary this brisk fall morning because someone had been impatient, and someone else had been drinking vodka in his morning orange juice. The two together had proved to be a deadly combination.

One young man, sober but impatient, had taken umbrage over a driver who insisted on driving slower than the posted limit, and who was weaving back and forth over the double line of the two-lane highway.

The other driver, an older male, had fortified himself with alcohol for the trip past the mountain park. His blurred mind, and slowed reflexes, were the cause of his erratic journey.

And then there had been the 'idiot' behind him, honking his horn, and flashing his lights. The drunk had gestured, and slowed even more.

Against all reason, his pursuer had decided that it was

wiser to pass then, than to wait for the lane to widen to two, a little later on. He had flashed his lights one more time, sounded his horn, and accelerated.

According to a number of badly shaken witnesses, as he had pulled level with the drunk, rounding a bend, a tanker truck, loaded with gasoline, came in the other direction.

The resulting crash had obliterated the car.

There had been no more need to rush after that.

The coroner made a cursory examination of what was left of the two men. From the looks of it, one had died on impact. The other had probably done the same when he hit the rocks, but he might have died from the fire. Only an autopsy would give the answer.

The firefighters had been on the site since the accident, washing down the road and trying to soak up fuel that had leaked from the tanker. Fortunately, the driver was only shaken up when his much heavier vehicle was struck by the little import. The truck had remained upright. The slow flow of fuel from the trailer had been stopped and another tanker was on the way, to drain the remaining gasoline.

The doctor was about to give his final clearance to the ambulance drivers when his pager sounded. He looked at the message on its screen and hustled on stubby legs back to his vehicle.

He reached in through the window, grabbed up the microphone, and called in. He was informed that there was a body in one of the downtown office buildings.

"It looks like foul play," the dispatcher told him. "How soon can you get there? They're in sort of a hurry."

"I'll get back as soon as I can."

He looked at his watch, and then at the line of slow-moving vehicles that trickled past the accident scene.

"I'll have to fight the commuter traffic, even with the lights and siren," he continued. "Tell them to hang tight."

The coroner walked slowly back to the ambulance by the side of the road. The EMTs were sitting on the back step of their truck. They both stood when they saw him approaching.

"Once you've finished bagging the two victims, take them to the morgue. I'll be tied up with something else for a while. One of my assistants will help you with signing them in."

The two men responded with nods of their heads, and turned to remove a gurney, and body bag from the ambulance.

Returning to his own transportation, the doctor fumbled for the key ring he had stuffed over the sun visor when he arrived. He selected the one for the ignition and started the SUV. The traffic was moving very slowly this morning.

Jack had expected that his friend needed help with a problem. When he saw the police presence, he had assumed that something serious had happened. A murder in your office would certainly be a cause for alarm.

But Jack had not suspected, for a moment, that the problem Brendan had was that he was assumed to be the perpetrator. He was dumbfounded. He thought that he probably looked a little comical standing by the reception counter with his mouth open.

Chief Detective Brown was still speaking.

"Problem is, he swears he's never seen the girl before. Nobody else around here seems able or willing to identify her either. Hopefully when the coroner gets here, we can begin to sort that out too."

"Jeez. What's holding him up today?" Jack asked.

"Major MVA up the highway. Four or five cars from what I've heard. Everybody's been kind of tight-lipped about it though."

"Sorta like the cops, eh Ted."

Jack went looking for Brendan Biggs.

He found his friend sitting in his office. It was obviously the workplace of a man with executive privileges. No expense had been spared to make it as comfortable as possible. The room was outfitted with fine leather chairs. A long couch dominated most of one wall. Brendan Biggs' desk faced a window that extended from ceiling to floor. It offered a panoramic view of the harbor, a block away. The advertising executive was not looking impressed by his elegant surroundings on this particular day. He was slumped with his head in his hands, his back to the door. He did not notice when his visitor came in.

Jack approached the desk, being careful not to startle his friend.

"Tough start to the day, Brendan?" he asked quietly.

Biggs' face came out of his hands, and he turned toward the voice. His eyes appeared unfocused and there wasn't the usual look of recognition at the sight of someone he had known since high school. He looked ten years older than the forty-something that he actually was.

"Yeah. Hi Jack. It's been bad so far. They tell me it could get worse. I don't know how much worse it could possibly be. They think I'm the one responsible. I haven't the slightest clue who that woman is."

Brendan gestured toward the open door, and the area beyond.

"Sit down," he continued. "We need to talk. Make sure you're comfortable. You may be here a while."

He backed his chair away from the work center and swiveled to face his friend.

Jack had always liked the wingback chair Brendan kept to the right of his desk. It was deeply padded and covered in burgundy leather, with a texture that the advertising company of Biggs, Wilberforce, Hutton, and Small would likely have called 'butter.' The idea of a long time spent discussing the problem at hand made Jack even more enamored of that particular piece of furniture. He was still feeling the aftermath of the previous evening's celebrations. He would appreciate the high back and the side support for his aching skull. He settled into the chair and let himself sink into its overstuffed interior. Its cushions gave a soft wheeze as they adjusted to the weight of their occupant.

"Fill me in. What are they saying and why?" Jack said.

"I stayed late last night. I was the last one out. I did some paperwork and locked up. I left later than I had intended. I got a little distracted and forgot about the time. I was supposed to see a client to finalize a contract, but he wasn't there. I haven't had the opportunity to call him this morning, to find out where he was. The cops see this as having the opportunity to commit the crime.

"I was here—alone. They figure she was killed after everyone else was gone. I guess I'm the logical suspect, but I swear to you, I was looking for my client on the other side of town. When he didn't show, I went home."

Jack leaned toward his friend, and surveyed his face carefully. Brendan's words brought a wrinkle to the private investigator's brow.

"The coroner still has to have his say in all this. Maybe he'll come up with something that will take the focus off you. You swear you've never seen this woman ever before?"

"Jack, I'd be willing to take a lie detector test on that one. I have no clue who she is, or why she would be here."

"When did you leave last night?" Jack asked.

"I finished up the paperwork and headed to the garage just after nine. I took the elevator right down to the parking lot so, unfortunately, I don't even have the security guard at the front desk to back up my alibi."

"It looks like we're going to have a real job ahead of us, if you're going to be absolved of this murder," Jack said.

"You used the word 'we.' Are you saying you'll help?"

"Hey, I've got nothing else to do today. How much effort could it possibly take? We'll have you off the hook in no time."

The truth was that Jack had begun to think he was going to have his hands full for some time to come. The ex-cop knew something of the procedures involved in dealing with a murder. In fact, Jack had been noted for his quick mind, and problem-solving skills while he was on the force. He had always seemed to be one step ahead of everyone else on the force when it came to rooting out evidence. The one time he had not been thinking fast enough had resulted in his expulsion from a job he loved.

During his years with the force, the homicide investigations he was involved with had been simple cases involving bad drug deals or marital disagreements. None of them had involved him emotionally. None of the suspects had ever been someone he actually knew. He wondered whether he would be able to look at the case objectively and sort out truth from fiction. He was fairly certain that his old friend wasn't involved with the death of this woman but then, how many times had he seen the darker, hidden side of people's lives before? He had delivered summonses and lawyers' letters to folks who, from the outside, looked like model citizens. Over the years, he had had to arrest lawyers and judges, bankers, and priests when he was an officer of the law. What made him so sure that Brendan Biggs, the advertising executive, was any less likely to have a hidden side?

Conversation filtering into Biggs' office from the work area indicated that the coroner had finally arrived and was beginning his investigation. Jack expressed his intention to join the others and Biggs rose to go with him.

"I'm hoping this nightmare will soon be over, Jack. I'm afraid of what may happen to me if I'm arrested. The bad publicity would be devastating to the company. For sure, my name would be peeled off the wall."

Brendan pointed to the company name, written in large brass letters opposite his office. "I don't expect to let it get that far, my friend. If you are as innocent as I suspect you are, the thought of dropping you from the partnership won't even cross anyone's mind. Trust me."

Jack wished he could trust his own words. He just didn't know for sure whether he could really help.

The two men moved toward the tightly huddled group watching as the coroner made his examination.

Only the police detectives, the EMTs, and a couple of uni-formed officers were left. Someone had arranged chairs and a couple of coat racks as a makeshift fence around the area where the body still lay. Yellow police tape had been tied to these.

Jack held down one of the flimsy barricades and stepped over it liker a boxer entering the ring for a fight. He bent down beside the short, heavy-set man who had a pair of wire-rimmed glasses perched on the end of his nose.

"Hiya Doc. Haven't seen you in awhile. How's it going?"

The man turned away from his investigation and toward Jack. A flash of recognition crossed his face.

"Hello. I remember you. You're with the city police," the coroner said.

"Used to be. I'm on my own right now. I do a little private investigation on the side. Can you tell me any more about what we've got here?"

Jack could see Keegan Willis out of the corner of his eye. The detective made a move, as if to bring the interrogation to an abrupt conclusion. Chief Detective Brown put out a firm hand to arrest his partner's forward movement, and mouthed, "It's okay."

"Not much," the coroner said. "I just got here. Can't tell you any more than what you can see with your own eyes. I'll know a little bit more after I'm finished with this prelim."

He looked at Jack with an expression that seemed to indicate that the process would go more swiftly if he was not disturbed while he was trying to do his job.

Dr. Lawrence Walle had been the coroner for three years. He had started his medical career as a GP twenty-five years before that. He had paid his dues as a family physician in a little farming village, patching broken legs and sewing up lacerations. Occasionally he had had to rescue an unfortunate soul from the jaws of a combine, or an encounter with some other piece of farming equipment. He had seen enough dismembered bodies, both alive and dead, that the transition to coroner was not much of a stretch. Now, of course, all his patients were dead.

He had a habit of reflecting on his past experiences in social situations. Jack had heard some of the stories and was convinced that the doctor wasn't likely to encounter anything he hadn't had to handle already. The only difference was that some of the dismemberments were intentional, and sometimes the victims purposely brought death upon themselves and grief to their families.

Jack stood up and moved toward his friend, whom he had left outside the cordoned-off area. Brendan was in conversation with the two detectives who stood just inside the tape. He was again protesting his innocence.

"I can assure you, officer, that I do not know this woman. I've never seen her before. I have no idea how she got in here. I locked up before I left. The office was empty when I went out."

Keegan Willis looked unimpressed. Chief Detective Brown was noncommittal, in either word or expression.

Jack took Biggs' arm and steered him away from the group. His face reflected his displeasure with Brendan's persistent speech.

"Brendan, you've got to trust me on this. If you keep on talking to those guys, they'll likely become more convinced that you had something to do with this. You haven't been officially charged."

He resisted adding the word "yet," though it was sitting at the back of his mind.

"Just try to keep your mouth shut," he continued. "Stay in your office. If they want you, they'll know where to find you. You might want to be looking up the number of the company lawyer, just in case."

Jack took his friend's arm firmly and turned him away from the investigation. Biggs slunk back to his office, looking like a beaten dog. The heavy wooden door closed behind him. Jack could visualize his friend thumbing through his Rolodex for the number of the law firm that the partnership kept on retainer.

Chapter Five

Brendan walked to his desk and looked out the window. Below him, the city was going about its business.

Out there, everything seemed to be moving along as it always did. The world was oblivious to what was happening eleven floors above.

In the offices of Biggs, Wilberforce, Hutton, and Small, and within Brendan Biggs, there was nothing but chaos. His life was in a shambles. If that window were not made of break-resistant material, he thought, he might have considered jumping out into the street below. *Stupid. That won't solve anything, other than bringing one investigation to a screeching halt—not to mention the traffic—and initiating another.*

It was best to stand his ground, Brendan decided.

Cooperate with the police. Answer their questions. No. Probably not that. Not without proper legal council. Jack was right. Best to warn the lawyers that they might be needed.

He reached for his card file and began thumbing through

it for the number of Horowicz, Kramner, and Horton, attorneys-at-law.

"Oh, jeez, I've got to get a new pair of knees. These ones are just about done."

Dr. Walle struggled to rise from his squatting position over the body. There was an audible crunching as his legs tried to propel the barrel-shaped torso into an upright position. He put away his pen and flipped open his notebook.

"Alright, boys, this is what I can tell you so far," the coroner began. "You already know it's a girl. She's been stabbed at least five times.

"She's been here since late last night, by the looks of it," he continued. "Liver temp indicates she may have died about a dozen hours ago, maybe more. I don't see any signs of great struggle.

"She has one defense wound on her right palm. Threw up her hand when she saw the knife coming. The first penetration likely ended her struggle. I think one of the wounds punctured her aorta. She's got other injuries that would have been equally fatal, but that one was probably what ruined her chances of survival.

"Everything after that was just insurance," the doctor said. "Whoever did this either wanted her dead or was in such a fit of anger they couldn't control themselves. She likely knew who her attacker was. I can't tell you more until I get her into my lab.

"It's too bad folks were so concerned to preserve her dignity this morning," he continued, with a look of genuine regret. "We might have some trouble separating out the forensic evidence from the stuff left from the blanket and DNA from the folks who were only trying to help. We'll have to do what we can."

The doctor stooped again and began packing his gear. The uniformed officers conferred briefly and headed for the reception area.

"You ambulance guys. I think we're ready to move the body. Take it easy. The doc here is going to want things disturbed as little as possible," the chief detective said to the EMTs.

"Ambulance guys. Thanks a bunch Mr. Policeman," one of them muttered under her breath. The other smiled and snapped on his rubber gloves before stooping to start the process of moving the body.

Soon the dead girl was bundled in a body bag, lifted up on the gurney, and strapped down for the trip to the morgue. The EMTs negotiated their way around cubicles and between desks and rattled out into the hallway.

Detective Willis reached into his wallet and pulled out a card. He offered it to Jack.

"Here. Give this to Mr. Biggs. They'll come in and clean up the mess. Have the place in working order by morning. We've got some samples, and the doc will be checking his stuff. Let him know we'll be in touch."

He indicated that 'he' was Biggs, with a nod in the direction of the executive's office.

Willis and Brown left.

At some point Jess and Abba had left too. All the others had vacated the building once it was clear that they couldn't be in on the action in the office.

Jack was left alone with his thoughts and the red stain on the carpet. He could hear Biggs talking on the phone behind his door.

Jack knocked gently and cracked the door open. Biggs turned toward his friend and motioned him in. Jack resumed his place in the wingback chair.

"No, I don't need you to do anything just yet. I'm just letting you know that I may need you to represent me if this thing goes sideways," Brendan said, into the receiver. "I have nothing to hide.

"Okay, I'll refer any of their questions to you," he continued. "Yes, I'll let you know how things turn out."

It was obvious to Jack that the lawyer was trying to keep his client from doing anything incriminating, or saying anything stupid. It was advice Jack would give him too.

When Brendan hung up the phone, Jack leaned closer. His brow wrinkled with concern.

"Brendan, you've got to be absolutely honest with me, if I'm going to try to help. I'm not a cop anymore. I'm not a lawyer. I know a little about both, and what they are going to want to do. Is there anything I should know?"

"I don't think so, Jack. Certainly I can't think of anything that relates to what we've seen here today."

"Who has keys to this place?"

"Well, of course, each of the partners, but I'm the only one in town. The employees have their own keys. We need to be able to get in to access the computers and the files whenever there is a client to satisfy. The cleaning company has a key."

"You mean the guys that clean the building?" Jack asked.

"No. We don't use them. We contracted with a private firm to do just our place. We wanted to make sure we could trust them. It costs a little more but these guys are bonded and have a good track record."

"Would someone have come in last night?"

"Oh, I would imagine so. They are usually in about ten o'clock. Work for an hour or so depending on how much traffic has been through here and then check out. They're signed in at the security desk downstairs when they come in. They're supposed to check out too."

"Supposed to?" Jack raised an eyebrow.

"Sometimes the guard is doing his rounds when the cleaners finish. If he's not at the desk, the guy is supposed to sign himself out. Sometimes he forgets."

"I'll have to check that out. Anything else I should know?"

"Don't think so. What do we do now?"

"Well, first of all, you sit tight. Do not say another word to the police. You don't know who they have spoken to or what additional evidence they might have.

"Especially don't talk to that Willis guy. He's a good cop but, when he gets an opinion in his head, it takes a little convincing to make him give it up. Right now, from what I can see, you don't have anything that will change his mind about you."

The two men sat looking at each other for a moment. Silence filled the room. Outside the window the wail of an ambulance could be heard eleven floors below.

"It's after noon. You hungry?" Brendan asked.

"I could use something about now, I guess. You buying?" Jack asked.

"Okay, let's go. I'll buy if you promise not to talk about this business during the meal. I'm nervous enough. I don't need anything else playing with my digestive system."

"Deal," Jack said.

He wouldn't talk. That didn't mean Jack wouldn't have to think. Who was the woman? No one seemed to know. If it was just as Brendan said, and if none of the office staff were lying, what was she doing in the office at night, and why did someone kill her? More important, who stabbed her to death?

Questions circled about, like vultures seeking the solution to their hunger, as Jack stood with his friend, waiting for the elevator. He pushed the 'down' button one more time and stared at the numbers, wondering if he would find answers to feed his curiosity about this new challenge.

The men spent a quiet lunch in the little steakhouse that overlooked the main street. From its broad front window, they watched the people walking by on their way to and from work. The passing parade also included shoppers, college students and, occasionally, bands of young people, apparently wearing the uniform of their particular gang.

These latter looked rough and angry. Sometimes they shouldered their way through the lunch hour crowd with evident unconcern for politeness. Jack wondered whether some of these might know what had happened the night before.

True to his word, he avoided any talk about the bloody scene they had left three blocks, and eleven stories away. Instead, they talked about their favorite sports teams and Jack's love life, or lack of one.

The men turned down the dessert menu. They asked for more coffee. Brendan paid the bill and they started their walk back to the offices of Biggs, Wilberforce, Hutton, and Small.

"Tell me," Jack asked. "Where are Wilberforce, Hutton, and Small? I don't believe I've met them. I didn't see their offices upstairs either."

"That's easily explained. Their offices aren't here. We are one of four branches that handle advertising. I'm low man, believe it or not. I get my name up front to compensate for a smaller cut of the profits."

"So, you're saying they each oversee an office in another city?"

"No, that's not quite true. They administer the whole affair from the head office in Toronto. I'm the odd guy out, I guess. They drop in, usually during the winter months, to 'show the flag,' but mostly to golf on the West Shore. We hardly see them much otherwise. Maybe these new developments will get their attention."

"I sure hope not," Jack said.

When the two men arrived back at the building where Brendan had his offices, the cleaning truck was pulled up by the main entrance.

The guard at the desk informed them that all the police had left, and that the clean-up crew had arrived about half an hour before. There was a message for Brendan that the office would have to be kept closed for the rest of the day. The regular cleaning crew would not be needed after the special team had finished their work. There wouldn't be anything that would require cleaning after they were done.

Brendan said he would take care of calling the regular janitorial service and telling them of the situation. He would call from the lobby and let the folks upstairs get about the task of removing all signs of the crime.

"I guess I'll head back to the office then," Jack said. "I'll need to give some thought to the facts of the case. Then, I guess I'll have to make some phone calls. I hope the coroner can shed some new light on the subject."

"I'll let you know if I think of anything that might help," Brendan said. "I appreciate your coming in on this. I know the police will be investigating but, since they're suggesting I'm the prime suspect so far, I know they've got that part wrong. I hope you can get me out of this soon."

"I'll do what I can."

Jack shook his friend's hand firmly, and then crossed to his car. There was a parking ticket on the windshield.

"I wonder if Brendan is paying expenses?" he asked himself as he got in and started the engine.

As Jack drove home, thoughts of the last time he had driven the westward route came to mind. Something had struck him as strange as he was heading home, almost ten hours earlier. What was it that was bothering him now? His fatigue, at the time, had dulled his reasoning. And that early in the morning he had had no reason to believe that the day would turn out as it had. Whatever it was would come to him, he was sure, but he wanted it right now. It wasn't responding to his call.

He drove across the bridge again, noticing that the rush hour traffic had not yet started. Another half hour and this road—the old highway—and the four-lane freeway a little to the north, would be jammed with office workers and laborers anxious to be home and getting angrier by the moment, because they were getting no closer. Jack hoped that once he got back to his office there would be a parking spot close by. He didn't like leaving the car in a place where he couldn't see it. Even though it was old, there were folks who would willingly steal it. He liked to find his stuff where he left it.

Fortunately, as he rounded the curve in the road, just before the old building, he saw that there was a spot that looked just large enough for him to squeeze into, right in front of the door. This would necessitate turning the car around to get on the right side. Jack shoulder-checked for his maneuver and seeing no representatives of the local constabulary, pulled a U-turn in the middle of the block. He waved enthusiastically at the driver of the car that had been coming towards him just before he had entered his sharp left turn. The other car's horn sounded a lengthy greeting and the driver made a gesture with his hand that Jack was sure he was fortunate not to have seen clearly.

After securing the vehicle, he headed upstairs to the office and looked in. The cream colored enamel was chipping from the wall in spots. The wainscoting was reminiscent of earlier days. His old desk was piled with papers in no particular order. The chair tilted to one side and one of the wheels was jammed just like those on the grocery carts at the supermarket back towards town. An old filing cabinet sat against the wall, its drawers so full that they would not close properly, nor open on occasion. The old Regulator clock had ceased to keep time. Jack knew the key was in his desk somewhere, but other things were more pressing right now. No messages on the answering machine. No mail under the door. All was well with the world if you didn't count the murdered girl downtown and the suspicion of Brendan's complicity.

Jack slumped in his chair. Still wearing his coat, he grabbed a sheet of paper and asked himself, "What do we know for sure?"

Almost everything Jack knew gave rise to more questions. Who was the victim? He hoped the coroner could sort that one out. Maybe she had some identification on her. The police wouldn't have told Jack, even if they knew, for the same reason they wouldn't want anyone else to know before next of kin had been contacted. What was she doing in the office? If it was true that no one knew her, she had no reason to be there, unless she had some unlawful purpose. That wasn't clear. Who killed her? And why? Where was the weapon? The police had not located it in the office complex.

Jack's head was beginning to ache again. Maybe a good night's rest would help to clear his mind. Maybe tomorrow would provide some more answers.

Maybe he was just fooling himself.

Chapter Six

It was late at night or early in the morning. Jack couldn't tell which. Before going to bed, in the hope of getting some much needed rest, he had again carefully placed the alarm clock so he couldn't see the time. It hadn't really mattered. He couldn't sleep.

Thoughts continued to circulate in his brain. Questions with no answers came to invade his time of rest. There was no other way for it but to get up.

He swung slowly out of bed and shuddered as his feet hit the cold, uncarpeted floor. He scratched unashamedly and looked at the clock. Eleven-nineteen. The night shift would have been at Brendan's office for just over three hours now. Maybe there were some answers behind the front desk. It was worth a try. Traffic would not be a problem at this hour.

Jack picked up his clothes from the floor, where he had thrown them before rolling into bed, an hour or so earlier. They would do for now. They were hardly soiled at all.

He dressed and headed downstairs.

I drive this road so often, this car could probably do this on its own, he thought as he drove the empty road into the center of town.

Jack knew that was not strictly true. He had tested the possibility once, quite late one night. That time, he had taken his hands off the steering wheel, and almost wiped out a light standard, when the vehicle had failed to take the bend to the right.

As he parked across the street from the darkened office building, Jack could see the night watchman sitting behind the desk in the lobby.

Here Biggs, Wilberforce, Hutton, and Small transacted business with people who had a product or service to sell and who wanted it to sell well. He knew after his earlier conversation with Brendan, that here at least, it was just Biggs who had been doing business on a day-to-day basis. But if Jack couldn't sort out some of the questions, even Brendan Biggs wouldn't be here.

The guard was leaned back in his chair, with his feet on the desk. Jack couldn't imagine how that could possibly be part of the job description for someone who was expected to be on the alert for strange happenings in the middle of the night.

Let's see how observant you've been, Jack thought of the guard.

When he rapped on one of the large windows, the resulting thunderous noise made the watchman startle and sit up. Jack had to smile, as he watched the man's feet come quickly off the desk to the floor.

The watchman looked across the lobby and out into the street to see the private investigator waving on the other side of the glass. He gave Jack a sharp chin up motion that asked,

"What are you doing, knocking on my window at this hour of the night?"

Jack pointed toward the locked door with one hand, and made the gesture of turning a key with the other. The guard made no great effort to get across the lobby in a hurry. As he came toward the entrance, he fumbled with a large ring of keys.

It surprised Jack how quickly the man found the right key and did what the night visitor had suggested.

Having unlocked the door and opening it only slightly, the guard inquired, "Who the heck are you, and what do you want? We're closed."

Obviously an ambassador for the city's tourist bureau, Jack thought.

He introduced himself and explained through the crack between the door and the jamb, that as a fellow representative of the forces of good, he was seeking the expertise of this alert gentleman in determining what goings-on might have transpired in this fine edifice on the evening of the alleged crime. Those weren't his exact words and he felt that if they had been the guardian of the door might simply have relocked and walked away. Somehow he convinced the man in the brown uniform to let him in and to at least talk about the previous evening.

It was evident that loneliness and the boredom of the job made the guard more than happy to converse on any subject at length.

His name was Graham and he had been at this job for almost two years now. Yes, he had been on duty the night before. Yes, he was familiar with the arrangements that the advertising firm had with the cleaning company.

"What do you remember about last night? Jack asked.

"Not much."

Jack's eyebrows went up at that statement.

"Well, what I mean is that there wasn't anything really extraordinary to speak of. Like I told the officers, things seemed like usual. That's why I was so surprised to hear the story on the radio about that girl getting whacked."

He leaned back in his chair, put his feet on the desk, and laced his fingers behind his head. He had been interviewed by Brown and Willis, he said, and had taken an instant disliking to the younger man.

"That fella just takes away my desire to volunteer anything, other than answers to what he asked. I was glad to see him go," he offered.

Looking over at Jack, he continued.

"I hear they had pictures on TV and everything. I never watch TV. Don't have time. I've got kids to take care of until the wife gets home from her job, and then I've gotta get ready to come here so I can add a little money to the bank account."

"Um, Graham, could I ask you to try and focus on last night. I'd sort of like to be on my way as soon as possible and let you get back to your work."

Jack was sure this exercise would make him ready for sleep.

"Sure. Ask away," Graham said, with enthusiasm.

"Okay. First off, did you see Mr. Biggs last night?"

"You mean the head advertising guy? Yeah. I didn't see him come in. I guess he was already here when I arrived, just before nine."

"Did you see him leave?"

"Yep. Around nine-twenty he came out of the elevator over there and let himself out. He has his own key. Parks down the block. I guess he went to his car. He looked a little agitated."

The guard rubbed his nose vigorously with the back of his

hand and sniffed loudly as he inspected his palm for foreign substances.

"How do you mean?"

"Well, he was looking at his watch and looking around the lobby and seemed real distracted. Know what I mean?"

"So that was before or after the cleaning crew arrived?"

"Guy."

"What?"

"Guy. Cleaning guy. Just one of 'em. Came after the head guy left."

"Is that all there is, usually?" Jack asked.

"Usually there's a bunch of 'em, but there was only one last night. New fella. Not very talkative."

"What did he look like?"

"Little ol' guy. Short. Wearing coveralls and a cap. Just came to the desk and said he was coming to clean the office up there. Looked a little lost, if you want to know. He signed the book and went on his way."

Graham's gaze went toward the high ceiling of the lobby and his eyelids began to droop.

"What about ID?" Jack asked, incredulous. "Did you check, to see if he was who he claimed to be?"

Graham's head snapped around and his eyes focused on Jack.

"Well, no. I guess I shoulda, but I was, you know, expecting to see someone from the cleaning company. When he showed up, I just sorta assumed he was . . ."

"Can I see the book?"

"Yeah, I guess."

The guard lowered his feet to the floor, opened a drawer in the desk, and pulled out a ledger. He opened it to the last page that had been written on and ran his finger down the column until he came to an entry.

"Here it is," he said, "Western Express Cleaning. No name, though. Came in at 9:40 P.M. Signed out at . . ." He paused, running his finger under the entry.

"Got a problem?" Jack asked, coming around the desk to look at the book.

"He must have forgotten to sign out. Could have been when I was doing rounds, I suppose. Regular guys are pretty good about doing their own sign-outs if I'm not here. I guess he didn't know the drill."

"Probably came through when I was doing my ten-fifteen check."

"You never saw him leave?"

"Nope." The watchman looked nearly as confused as Jack felt.

"How would he get out? Isn't the door locked?"

Graham raised a hand and pointed at Jack, a light of realization in his eyes.

"Now that you mention it, that's true. Unless . . ."

"Unless what?"

"Unless he took the elevator clear to the basement. They sometimes leave the truck in the carpark."

"Which way did he come in last night? Out of the elevator from downstairs?"

"No. I had to let him in, I remember 'cause Mr. Big locked it when he went out."

"Biggs," Jack corrected him.

"Whatever."

"Did you see his truck?"

"Uh, no. But, if he parked it downstairs . . ."

"He would have come up the elevator," Jack said.

"Yeah, I guess you're right. Weird."

"What kind of equipment did he bring with him?"

"Jeez. You know. He didn't bring anything in with him.

When they park downstairs, they leave their cart in the elevator. One guy holds the door while someone signs in for the crew.

"He walked in off the street and I don't remember him having anything with him at all." The guard looked genuinely confused by the realization.

"Could you identify him if you saw him again?"

"To be honest, I don't know. I can't say I paid a lot of attention to the guy. I figured he was here on regular business."

Graham was beginning to look a little fearful of the possibility that he might have failed at doing his job.

"Well, I think I've heard enough for tonight. I can see I've got a little more investigating to do. Would it be all right if I came back another time, if I have any more questions?"

The guard shrugged. "Suits me. I'm usually right here, unless I'm not. I mean, unless I'm doing my rounds. If you don't see me, I'll be back here within the next three-quarters of an hour. Takes about that much time to check the doors and get back down."

"One more thing," Jack said.

"Yeah?"

"Can I have a look at the surveillance tapes?"

A smile crossed Graham's tired face.

"I'll tell you what I told your police buddies," the guard said. "If I had some, I'd let you have 'em. But, there's no cameras here, except one place."

"Where's that?" Jack asked.

"Through those doors," the guard said, pointing toward the lobby of the bank across the foyer.

"This place isn't one of the newest buildings in town," he continued. "The bank put in their own stuff and run a tape. Your money disappears overnight, you can watch it happen the next day."

Graham's countenance took on a look of regret that Jack thought might be because of the lack of evidence. It was not.

"If we had proper surveillance cameras," the watchman continued, "I wouldn't have to take all those long walks, in the corridors, at night. I'd just sit here in my 'command center." He made quotation marks with his fingers. "I could watch the place from here and save my legs."

It was Jack's turn to sport a look of regret. He wondered whether the building manager was fully aware of what he was, and wasn't, getting for his money.

He thanked the security guard, and was let out onto the sidewalk again. By the time he crossed the street and unlocked his car, Graham was back at his 'command center' with his feet on the desk.

Jack had more questions to deal with than when he started, it seemed.

He hoped he was tired enough to get to sleep this time. His conversation had left him drowsy. Maybe he'd function better after some rest. But the questions the watchman had raised in his mind were going to plague his sleep.

Rest, it would turn out, was going to be in short supply for some time to come.

Chapter Seven

J ack went straight to bed. He had to get some sleep, or he would be no use to his friend. Of course, he wasn't sure that he could be any help, unless he could find some convincing evidence that would make the police take the spotlight off Brendan.

He lay in bed staring at the ceiling. He would need to make a trip to the cleaning company offices. *Was it possible to prove his friend was not in the building when the murder took place?*

Jack needed to talk to Brendan's possible alibi. He would need to track down the client his friend claimed had not shown up for the meeting he said had been arranged.

The coroner's time of death estimate would have to be confirmed. Maybe once the body was identified, things would begin to come together.

Jack slept fitfully until eight the next morning. He didn't have a lot of time to spare before he needed to talk to Dr. Walle in his cold little lab, in the basement of police headquarters. Jack was glad of his former connections. He couldn't imagine how difficult it would be for any other civilian to get into the inner sanctum of the city cops.

He was hoping it wasn't being presumptuous to think that he would be allowed into the morgue. It would be worse than frustrating to be stonewalled at this early stage. He smiled at the unintentional pun on the coroner's name.

Jack drove through the center of town, picking his way through the throngs of people going back and forth across the intersections. Folks weren't always careful to abide by the rules and assumed that since they were on foot, they always had the right of way, even if the traffic signals said otherwise. Some of those who felt that Jack should not attempt to go forward on a green light would show their unhappiness, in word and action, as he attempted to thread his way through the open spaces between the boulevards.

As he approached the police headquarters, the pedestrian traffic diminished somewhat, and he noticed that other vehicles tended to obey the highway code more stringently when they were within sight of the building with its lot brimming with patrol cars.

He forced to the back of his mind a fleeting thought about the public perception that, at around ten o'clock, the lot would be almost empty, and the command center would be moved to the local doughnut shop.

He had been a law enforcement officer once. He knew that the job was one which didn't always get the respect it deserved. Jack remembered how the coffee shop jokes had made his own blood pressure rise, especially when there was a serious investigation being carried out. In a city this size, major cases were being dealt with on a daily basis. The fact that most people didn't recognize this, was testimony to the truth that the job was being well done. But that ignorance was what kept the jokes coming.

Jack pulled into the visitor parking lot, and managed to get into a spot, halfway down the row, before the old car's engine stalled. He got out and slammed the door, to make sure the latch caught on the first try. Looking around at the other vehicles in the lot, he reminded himself again, that cleanliness wasn't really next to godliness. When he bought his next car, it would be clean for at least a day.

Jack walked into the headquarters building and approached a young, uniformed female behind a window marked 'Information.' Her badge said simply, 'Grainger.' She looked up as he entered and smiled with perfect teeth.

"I'm here to see the coroner," he said, returning the smile but knowing his would never match the orthodontically enhanced Officer Grainger's.

"May I have your name, sir?"

Nothing made Jack feel that he had passed from his youth, to middle age, as quickly as a good-looking woman addressing him as 'sir.'

"Jack Elton. You can call me Jack." He added his best smile.

"Just a moment, sir."

There it was again—sir—and a row of perfect, white teeth.

I must look really bad today, he thought.

After a few inquiries on the phone, Officer Grainger directed Jack to a door to the right of her window. An electronic buzz sounded, indicating that the automatic lock was being deactivated, as he turned the knob. He was being granted access to an area where most folks would not be welcome, unless they were on serious business, or the police had some serious business with them. These latter usually did not have their hands free to turn the knob, and were assisted through the door with some degree of force or authority.

Jack walked down one side of the office area to a stairwell at the far end. A sign indicated that the crime investigations branch was up one more floor. An arrow directed him down to the basement, where Dr. Walle, and others like him, dealt with the bodies of those who had had the misfortune to become subjects of postmortem investigation.

Below the bright offices of the police department were the gray-walled cubicles with the stainless steel trolleys. A number of refrigerated drawers held evidence that the city was not always law-abiding, and death didn't always come peacefully, or only in old age. Jack had never enjoyed these trips, even when he had been a member of the force. The things that were done to the bodies that were brought here, even after they had already experienced indignities at the hands of others, were not pleasant subjects for conversation. Less so, the experience of seeing the results of autopsy. The fact that it had to be done did not make it any more palatable.

Jack was almost certain that Dr. Walle knew what had killed the girl in Brendan's office. He had found the knife wound and seen the blood. Nonetheless, a more official, external exam would have been performed and the information entered on the approved form.

Jack pressed a large metal disk on the wall beside the heavy double doors, and they sighed open to allow him into the morgue. The smell of death was distinct. Anyone who had experienced it would never forget it. Jack knew the odor and made a point to avoid it whenever possible. Today would not be one of those fortunate days.

He tried hard to control his breathing and a gag reflex that kept him from taking up forensic medicine as a vocation. He was glad he had not eaten since the night before.

Dr. Walle was hovering over one of the steel tables and talking into a hanging microphone as Jack approached. The doctor used a foot switch to turn off the tape recorder and laid down his instruments. The coroner pulled a sheet over the corpse and snapped off his rubber gloves into a covered waste receptacle with a red biohazard logo. He turned to the sink and began washing his hands.

A halo of white hair was illuminated by the operating lamp the doctor had turned askew before he moved from the table.

"You're here about that Jane Doe that was found downtown," he said, turning toward Jack. "I don't know that I can tell you much, but if you want to come into the office, I'll review my report with you, as much as I'm able. I don't ordinarily talk to people who are not with the police, but Detective Brown told me a little of your history. He asked me to help you as long as it doesn't compromise the police investigation."

He pulled down a wad of paper towel from a wall dispenser and dried his hands. The paper went into another covered container. He led Jack out of the lab to a small office, and indicated a chair for Jack to sit.

"Coffee?" he asked, holding up a cup, and the carafe from the machine on the counter, behind the desk.

"Yes, thanks. Nice little office you have here," Jack offered.

"It's a place I can retreat to when life gets depressing around here. It does that a lot in this business. Cream? Sugar?"

The doctor poured a mug of coffee for Jack, and another

for himself, and placed Tupperware containers of sugar and powdered creamer in the middle of the desk. Jack resisted the urge to make a face when he saw the coffee whitener. He was feeling adventurous and shook a little of the powder on the surface of the dark liquid.

"Do you have an ID for our lady of the eleventh floor yet?" Jack mashed at a lump of creamer floating on the surface of his coffee with a stir stick.

"We didn't find any identification among the few personal effects she was carrying. I've taken fingerprints, and we have dental impressions, but that's it right now."

Dr. Walle thumbed a folder he had picked up from his desk.

"Has anyone reported a missing person? Is there any indication that someone might be looking for her?"

"I'm sure that someone must be missing her. The problem is, she's an adult. It's not like she was a teenager whose parents would be looking for her, when she didn't come home after work. I don't think she was married. She wasn't wearing a ring, and there is no indication that she ever had a ring on that finger. No indentations. No tan lines.

"That's not to say she wasn't behaving like she was married, if you catch my drift," the doctor added.

Jack caught exactly what the good doctor was implying.

"She might have been living with someone," Jack said.

"That's true, but so far no one is claiming her. She must have had a relationship with a man, however brief, within the last two or three months, though. She was pregnant."

"So someone will surely claim her."

"Depends."

"On what?"

"If she was still on good terms with the guy, and if he was willing to accept responsibility for the pregnancy, we might hear from him. Otherwise, he might not even notice that she was gone. And there is one more thing besides."

"What would that be?" Jack stirred his coffee again and leaned closer to the desk.

"You might have noticed that she looked Asian? She was that. At least partly."

"And your point is . . ."

"In this city, we are dealing with a very close-knit community. Little of the tradition has changed for many of these folks. Getting information from some of her neighbors may be difficult. That she was pregnant may also have a stifling effect on how much information you'll be able to get."

"I think if we could establish some kind of motive we might be able to track down the perpetrator."

"Mr. Elton, if we can track down the perpetrator, we'll be able to establish the motive. You can go at it from either direction. Unfortunately, all we have right now is the end result. I'm no wiser than you at this point. I would hope that you will afford us the same courtesy as we have extended to you, if you come upon anything that will help."

The doctor drained his cup and placed it on the counter. The interview was over for now. The body in the lab needed attending to, it appeared.

"Doctor, I can assure you," Jack said, swilling the last dregs of coffee and undissolved creamer in his cup, "if I learn anything, I will make sure that you folks are in the loop. I want this solved as much as you do. I have a personal stake in this mystery being solved."

"Ah, yes. Your friend does seem to be carrying the weight of suspicion at this point. I try to stay out of the business of speculation myself. I've seen a case turn on the weight of the smallest piece of evidence. Now, I must get back to Mr. Baxter out there. You'll forgive me if I don't escort you back up-stairs." Dr. Walle held the door for Jack.

"I know the way. Thanks for your help. I'll be in touch." Jack walked back through the lab. Then he stopped and re-traced his steps.

"Just one more question before I go, Doctor. Can you give me a time of death?"

"You look like you'll last through the rest of the day, young man," the doctor replied. There was a twinkle in his eye.

"No. I meant the girl."

"I know. I know," the coroner said with a hint of disap-pointment in his voice that the visitor had missed the attempt at humor. "She died sometime between nine P.M. and eleven. That's the best I can do."

"It's a start," Jack said. "It'll do for now. Thanks."

Dr. Walle returned to the steel table and removed the sheet covering Mr. Baxter. He had not moved.

Jack stepped out into the mid-morning sunshine and breathed deeply. The odor of death seemed to cling to his clothes. It was good to be alive. It was better to be out of the morgue.

Chapter Eight

T he old car rattled back through town toward the advertising office, encountering the same irresponsible pedestrians that had hampered the trip to the police station. Jack had more questions for Brendan and felt it might be helpful to give some encouragement to his friend. He planned to report what he had been able to find out, during his middle-of-the-night investigation, and the little that Lawrence Walle had provided about the victim. It was frustrating him that he knew so little that would help, at least as far as the girl's identity was concerned.

Jack really wanted to help his friend, but it seemed there was no way to do that right now. There was a dead body. How she had died was known. He knew why Brendan was under suspicion.

The process of identifying a body required other details for comparison.

A family reports their daughter missing. They have a name, some pictures, and a description of what she was wearing. If she's alive and found, it's a simple matter. If she turns up dead, and it's soon enough, the outcome is much sadder, but you can, at least, figure out who she is. A while later, and you are going to need dental records. Or ID found on the remains, at a minimum.

This girl didn't seem to have anyone who cared enough to call police on her behalf. Her body was still intact or had been until Dr. Walle had done his work in the autopsy room. Still, there was no name, no documentation, and no records to which to compare tissue, blood, or teeth. She didn't match anyone reported missing in the recent past, either.

What else was there? Something was stirring at the back of his mind. Something he had seen or heard was tugging at his subconscious. What was it? And did it have anything at all to do with the struggle to get Brendan exonerated.

As Jack pulled up to the offices of Biggs, Wilberforce, Hutton, and Small, his blood ran cold at the sight before him. Outside the entrance to the building were two police vehicles; the unmarked cruiser he knew belonged to the detectives, and the city paddy wagon, ready for a passenger.

He hurried to park, and came to a stop with one wheel of the old car up over the curb. Without locking the car, he sprinted to the front doors of the high rise, and pushed through.

Dave Simpson, Jack's former partner, had been assigned to the task of guarding the lobby again. When he saw the private investigator run in, he made a note on his clipboard and, with a wave of his hand, signaled for him to go upstairs.

At the elevator, Jack stood impatiently, pressing the 'up' button repeatedly, as if that would hasten the conveyance's arrival. Once inside and on the way up to the eleventh floor, he shifted back and forth from foot to foot.

"This does not look . . . not good at all," he muttered to himself, shaking his head.

The elevator slowed to a stop. The doors started to open and he used both hands to force them apart. As he reached the entrance to the office, he could see that he wouldn't get a private moment with Brendan Biggs just yet.

He pulled open one of the glass doors.

". . . the right to remain silent. Anything you say can and will be used . . ."

Jack didn't have to hear the rest of Detective Willis' admonition to know what was happening. If there had been any doubt, the sight of Brendan in handcuffs confirmed his fears. Two officers flanked Jack's friend. Chief Detective Brown was looking serious. Willis was enjoying his job far too much. Brendan looked like he would probably need a clean change of underwear.

"We have no other choice, Jack. The evidence points strongly in Mr. Biggs' direction. There is other information, as a result of the ongoing investigation, that seems to implicate him further. We have no other suspects and my boss wants us to, at least, appear as if we're on top of things."

Brown had seen Jack's entrance, and had taken his cue from the look on the investigator's face. The two had worked together in the past and, although they didn't always see eye-to-eye on some things, they had always had a good relationship and tried to help each other out when the opportunity presented itself.

"Where's he going?"

"Downtown, to the central office. We'll hold him in the cells while we continue the investigation. The television and papers want to know what we're doing about this case, and I guess Chief Jaworowicz feels we should show them we take our suspects seriously."

Jack shook his head as the officers ushered their prisoner toward the hallway. It appeared that things were going from bad to worse.

Things always seem darkest just before everything goes completely black, he thought.

"Jack, get me out of this. You know I'm innocent. I wasn't even near here when this happened. You gotta believe me," Brendan called over his shoulder.

"I'll do everything I can. Just hold tight."

Jack wondered what he could do. He'd have to have a heart-to-heart with his friend 'downtown,' as they used to say in the old police shows on TV.

"We'll take care of him," the senior detective said, as he slipped around the edge of the reception counter, trailed by his partner.

Detective Willis gave Jack a look that made him glad that Brown was in command. Otherwise, he feared, Brendan might have had some sort of 'accident' in the cells while he was awaiting the wheels of justice to turn in his favor. Willis, unfortunately, was a loose cannon with a short fuse.

Jack waited for the elevator car to come back up. The advertising company had resumed business after a day of waiting for the preliminary investigations to be completed. He assumed that the clean-up crew that the police used in these cases had done its job and the spot on the carpet, and stains elsewhere, had been removed. In the excitement of the moment, he had not bothered to check. He made another mental note to himself, to contact the janitorial service that was under contract to the advertising company as soon as possible. He needed to track down the guy who had done the cleaning on the night of the murder. What had the man seen, and was he the one who had left the door unlocked?

Jack suspected that the answers might not be forthcoming until the murderer was caught. He was sure they were one and the same. He just needed to prove it.

Piece of cake. Piece of dry, flavorless, make-you-gag fruitcake.

A bell sounded softly and he stepped inside the elevator. As the doors came together again, he stabbed the button for the main floor and leaned against the side of the car. He ached all over, and a wave of fatigue swept over him. His mood was dropping like the elevator. Jack needed to think. He needed to take a walk.

Once on the ground level, Jack headed towards the main doors. He noticed, as he passed the security desk, that a young guard was standing by the wall looking attentive to all the comings and goings of the day.

A far cry from your buddy who works the night shift, he thought, as he stepped out onto the sidewalk.

The patrol car and other police vehicle had left, their duty done for now. He remembered that he had not locked his own car, and he crossed to where it was sitting.

Noticing his poor parking job, he got in and backed off the curb. Once he had assured himself that everything was secure, he started walking along the street and down the hill that led past the souvenir shops.

Jack pocketed the parking ticket that had been left on his window.

The day was bright, and the air was fresh. A warm sun shone on the city and, for the most part, people seemed happy. Jack was careful, as he walked, that he did not become one of those folks who had so provoked him when he had been driving earlier that morning. He stopped at red lights and did not venture to cross the street until the little walking figure appeared on the light signal across the intersection.

Jack soon discovered that his walking, or rather his waiting, could be as much provocation to other pedestrians as had been his legal use of the streets a few hours earlier. At more than one street corner, he was jostled and given unhappy side glances as he set a good example for those who did not care to have an example set for them. With each little push and shove, his hand verified that his wallet was still where it should be—in his pocket, and not someone else's.

The little bird that signaled a green light to the visually challenged had laryngitis.

The street looked different than it had three days ago, when he had been returning from that party, not as much in control of his vehicle as he should have been, owing to the somewhat higher level of alcohol in his system than usual for such an early hour.

The thoroughfares were populated with workers and tourists. Street people had taken up favorite spots against the sun-warmed fronts of the buildings. Some had dogs that lounged lazily beside them. The tourist shops were doing a brisk business. Sandwich boards proclaimed that this shop or that had the best deals in T-shirts or postcards. The higher class establishments advertised designer clothing or genuine Hudson's Bay blankets.

As Jack walked, he reflected on the past few days. It came to him suddenly what had struck him as unusual about what he had seen in this place two days earlier. There was probably a logical explanation. He would have to check it out later. Right now he had to find a way to get Brendan sprung from his 'cold prison cell.'

Even as he thought it, Jack knew that his friend was far from being in a stark cell. Oh yes, he was locked up, and he did have to wait until he could be bailed out. There would be enough paperwork to keep him occupied for a while yet, but the cells were bright and the air was warm. He couldn't imagine that Brendan would have to drag a tin cup back and forth over the bars to draw attention. He was probably sitting across a table from the two detectives right now while they filled in the stacks of forms required before things could go further. As Jack remembered, the coffee wasn't too bad either. Too bad they didn't have real cream. Prison would be more bearable otherwise.

At the foot of the hill, Jack turned west and headed over to the next block. Tourist buses and horse-drawn carriages competed for space with cars and trucks. A microcosm of the world's population crossed back and forth along the sidewalks. Folks came from all over to visit the city. As groups passed, he could hear people talking, sometimes excitedly, in languages he could not fathom. He wondered what they were saying to one another. He wondered what they would say if they knew that, just a couple of blocks away, a young girl, whose roots were also in another country, had had her life taken suddenly and brutally three days ago.

Right now, some pointed at the clock tower and explained how it had been a gift to the city some years ago. Jack assumed that was what they were saying. A group of Japanese tourists was being instructed by a young female guide, as they stood outside the museum. Others headed past the little harbor, where a passenger ferry came and went twice a day, taking folks across the strait to other adventures in tourism.

Jack had no time to stop and marvel at the wonders of his own city today. There were other, more pressing, matters to deal with. It occurred to him that he had never spoken to Brendan about getting paid for his work. While he was running around on behalf of his friend, he was neglecting his other business. Not that it was bringing in vast amounts of cash, even at the best of times, but the folks who usually hired him to deliver their legal papers knew that it would cost them. For the particularly sticky situations he had to face, Jack was able to exact a little extra for danger pay. It kept food on the table and some food in the fridge. Surely the finances of Biggs, Wilberforce, Hutton, and Small were sufficient to afford a substantial fee for his services.

Jack felt the parking ticket in his pocket. At the rate the city was charging him for parking, it could become very expensive. Maybe today wasn't the best day to discuss financial matters.

Chapter Nine

Back in his car, Jack sat for a moment contemplating his next move. His friend's release was, of course, a priority. That could take some time, as Brendan was run through the routine. Paperwork was always the problem. You had to get a guy signed in before you could get him released. The process worked in one direction only. There was no 'oops' factor built in, if you started a file and then discovered that you had the wrong person. You had to have the paperwork so you could write on it that a mistake had been made. Jack pounded the steering wheel as he remembered the frustration of the process. He dared not even think of the times he had been a party to the loss of incomplete forms, when it had become clear that a case needed to go in an other direction with completely different players.

Brendan's alibi was a sticking point. He said he was waiting for a business contact who never showed up. Was there no one who could corroborate his friend's story? Maybe the office cleaner could do that. Jack would have to get more details from his friend. And he would definitely need to speak to the folks at Western Express Cleaning. Problem was, he had no authority to ask. Would they be willing to put him in touch with their employee? Would the guy be allowed to speak about what he had or hadn't seen without a warrant of some sort?

Jack was beginning to regret the approach that had gotten him the reputation of a 'lone ranger' when he was on the police force. It haunted him now when he ached to be in several places at once.

Jack had gathered that Abba—he thought that was the name of the young girl in the office—had been the one to make the discovery. The office manager—what was her name? He couldn't remember. The office manager had made the call to the police. Maybe they knew something that would help. Maybe there were others in the office, who could vouch for their boss' whereabouts the night before.

He had to do something. He couldn't just sit and meditate on these things. Jack opened the door, and stepped out into the street again.

Across town, Brendan Biggs sat anxiously in the interrogation room. He bit on his lower lip as the two police detectives continued to ask their questions.

"You understand, Mr. Biggs, how we might have some difficulty believing your story. There are no witnesses to your leaving the building, except for the guard at the front door. And he can't even vouch for you, as far as exactly when you went past his station. Can you prove that you didn't return through the garage and, let's say, just for the sake of argument, take the elevator back up to your office with the girl?"

Brendan sat in silence.

Brown was keeping a businesslike demeanor. He could

see the terror in Brendan's eyes. As far as he knew, the man had never been in serious trouble with the law until now. He might be innocent, but procedures had to be followed. No use setting everyone up for trouble down the road.

Keegan Willis, on the other hand, was a student of the good cop/bad cop school of interrogation and never missed an opportunity to be loud and abrasive, when it suited him.

"Get real, Biggs. Let's make it easy on all of us. We can stay here for a good long time. Come clean and we might be able to cut you a deal. Tell us how you killed the girl—and why. Things will go a lot more smoothly if you don't give us any more grief. Why did you do it?"

He was close enough to Brendan's face at this point that the businessman could smell the stale coffee on his breath and see the scar on the detective's forehead caused, not from the perils of police work, but from a run-in with the edge of a garage door one dark night.

Unlike Brown, Willis was encouraged by Brendan's uneasy look. He hadn't bothered to check, but figured a guy like Brendan Biggs couldn't have got to where he was by honest means.

He's probably got a rap sheet as long as my arm, he thought as he closed in for another bombing run. In his mind, Brendan Biggs was guilty. Too bad they had to follow protocol.

Brendan went on the defensive.

"Look. I've told you everything I know. I was not in that office when the girl was killed. I swear, I don't know who she is—was."

"Can you prove you left at nine?" Brown asked.

Keegan Willis looked smug, waiting for Brendan to dig himself a hole.

Their suspect shifted uneasily, and looked thoroughly frustrated.

"I guess I can't. I had an appointment for nine o'clock. I got busy. I worked at my desk, and when I looked up, it was already past that time. I rushed out. I remember locking the door. I was anxious to meet my client. I didn't have time for pleasantries with the guard. I probably looked a little distracted to him. Wouldn't you be?"

"Weren't you just in a hurry to get away from a violent, bloody crime scene?" Willis asked through clenched teeth.

Brendan did not see Brown grab the back of his partner's shirt, and pull him back in his seat.

He replied, "No, I wasn't."

Back on the eleventh floor, Jack saw that it was essentially business as usual in the advertising agency. Of course, there was no telling what was going on inside the heads of these people. Underneath the business-like atmosphere, there might be lingering fear or sadness. Or guilt.

Jack found Abba in her cubicle, in the centre of the office. It was obvious she had just finished dealing with a client. Sketches of different presentations were spread over one side of her desk. A legal pad, covered with notes and doodles, lay on the desk blotter. Abba was gathering and sorting the papers into some semblance of order, and was labeling folders as she went. She looked up when Jack came to the entrance to her work space. A flicker of recognition crossed her face followed by a dark shadow.

"My name is Jack Elton. We met a couple of days ago. May I have a moment of your time?" he asked.

"Depends on what for. I remember you. I know the sorts of things you want to ask."

She wasn't angry, but it was clear she would have preferred to be doing other things.

"I'll try not to take too much time," Jack said.

"It's not the time I'm worried about. It's the idea of having to think about, you know . . ." Abba's voice trailed off, and she looked away from her visitor.

"Do you want to help Brendan, I mean Mr. Biggs?"

"It's okay. We all use first names around here. I call him Brendan. My name's Abba. You can call me Abby. That's what friends call me."

"Well, Abby, I certainly want to be your friend. You do want to try to help Brendan, then?"

"Oh yes." Her tone indicated that she had positive feelings for the boss. "It broke my heart to see the police take him away the way they did, with the handcuffs and all. I don't think he had anything to do with the . . . with the murder."

"I'm glad to hear you say that. Let's go back to that evening, when you left the office."

"Could you hold on for a second? I've got to get these papers filed and pass on some work to one of the other guys for a client. I'll be right back."

"Sure, Abby."

Abba walked across the office and stopped and leaned over the desk of a young man in another cubicle. She passed him one of the files and spoke animatedly to her co-worker. He responded in kind. They were smiling.

Jack watched as they talked, unable to make out what was being said.

A few moments later Abba returned to her desk and sat. Looking at Jack she leaned back, tenting her fingers in front of her mouth.

"Okay, shoot. What do you want to know?"

"It's important that you tell me everything you can remember from that night. The smallest detail can be helpful. What did you do before you left? Take as much time as you need."

"That's easy. I was here until about seven. I had been working on an account for one of our more important clients. I had to arrange some TV shoots for the next day. I was putting a package together for the client."

"So you were here, at your desk?"

"Yeah, most of the time. Like, I was back and forth to the file cabinets, the copier. The bathroom, if you really must know. But I was here. No one came in. Everyone else had left, except Brendan. He was in his office with the door closed."

With her hand, she indicated the door that was familiar territory to Jack.

"He was there when you left?" Jack asked.

"Absolutely. I knocked on his door to say I was leaving. He told me to come in. I opened the door and said good night. He said good night, and explained he would be leaving a little later."

"Is that usual, Abby?"

The woman though a moment before replying.

"Yeah, I'd have to say that he works late a lot of the time. Not every night, but at least a couple a week."

Jack reflected on a recent conversation he and Brendan had had, about his friend's home life.

Brendan had admitted that he and Meagan were having a few problems, after fifteen years of marriage. He hadn't gone into much detail, except to say that things were becoming a little strained lately. The marriage wasn't in any jeopardy, as far as he could tell. They were still living and sleeping together.

"Just a few problems from time to time," he had said.

Jack hadn't wanted to press for more information. With Brendan in the emotional state that he had been, it probably wasn't the best time to be probing into something that didn't seem relevant to the present situation. He'd made a mental note to ask about it at a later date. It had lain at the bottom of a heap of other mental notes that had fallen off the notice board of his mind in the past two or three days.

Jack was ready to bet that Brendan's work habits had something to do with the matrimonial strain.

"Tell me again what was happening that night," he continued.

"Okay. He had a meeting with a prospect. Big account. Didn't say who, or what their product was. He was going to take along some samples of stuff we had done. Magazines. TV. Newspapers. Direct mail. That sort of thing. Seemed pretty excited about the prospect. The appointment was for sometime around nine."

"Do you know where?"

"Nope. He was keeping all of that pretty close to the vest. Didn't want to let anything slip. It's a thing with him. He's afraid he'll jinx the deal if anybody knows what's happening."

"So you left when?"

"Like I said before, I was here till about seven, and then headed home. I took some work with me. It's just been real hectic around here."

"Everything seemed kosher when you left."

"Yes. Brendan was still working in his office. I turned off some of the lights. I picked up my files and left. Oh, yeah. I locked the door behind me. Brendan asked me to do that. Said he'd let himself out, and lock up, when he was through."

"So the door was locked when you left."

"That's right. I remember having trouble getting the keys back in my pocket, because I had the armload of files. I took the elevator down to the carpark and drove home. I was there all night. You can ask my cat."

She smiled at Jack, and played with a stray strand of her dark hair. He smiled back, glad that the clouded expression had cleared from her face.

Jack thanked Abba for her help and added that he'd be in touch if he had any other questions. She said she would do what she could.

"Say hello to Brendan for me, please, if you happen to see him," she said, as Jack stood to leave.

"I'll do that. I hope he'll be back here soon, so you can say hi to him yourself."

He turned and headed for the door. At least he had confirmation of the fact that his friend had been in the office that evening, but no support for an alibi.

Brendan could have stayed there, committed murder, and then slipped out and gone home. The trouble was that Brendan had said the appointment was at nine, but he had not passed the guard at the front desk until 9:20.

Jack needed to talk to the client his friend was supposed to see. In spite of the fact that the meeting never took place, the record of an appointment would at least give credibility to the ad man's claims. Biggs would have to break down and reveal who the prospect was.

"The plan is jinxed already, my friend. You might as well open up about it. It couldn't possibly get much worse," Jack said to the image of Brendan in jail that remained in his head.

Chapter Ten

"**S**uperSave Groceries. I was going to meet with the head of their advertising department, at the company office, over in the industrial park. They have a warehouse down there. The offices are on the second floor. I've already told the two detectives, but apparently there's no record of the appointment. I'm in real trouble, aren't I?"

Jack had gone from Brendan's office directly to the police headquarters, and had requested access to the cell where his friend was being held. He wasn't a lawyer or family but had managed to get in by dropping the names of a few folks higher up on the food chain. It helped, too, that he was not a stranger to the place. His face was recognized. So was his reputation, but it seemed that with time more people were beginning to believe he was trustworthy.

Now Jack sat on a steel chair, in the little room that was going to be home for Brendan until something could be found to prove his innocence. From what his friend was telling him, that task had just become more difficult.

"So you went over there at around nine to talk to this guy, Forbes. He's the guy who makes the final decision on who gets the advertising account."

"That's it. Garry Forbes was supposed to meet me there and we were going to go to his office, so I could show him our stuff. He was going to have a monitor and tape player set up, so I could show him some of the television ads we have done for other companies. We were meeting late because he has kids in basketball, or something, and he had to pick them up and take them home first."

"You left the office late. So what happened?"

"Like I said, I got tied up with my preparation for the meeting and lost track of time. I was really ticked with myself, let me tell you. And I had to park my car farther away than usual that morning."

"Okay, so you left the office and got to your car. You drove out to the warehouse. Then what?"

"I drove into their lot and parked by the door. The lights were out and I figured Forbes was probably delayed because a game ran long, or the traffic was slow. It rained that night, you remember. He's really careful about his kids. He told me that himself. Said, if I arrived and he wasn't there, I should just sit tight. Well, I did. He never came."

"So you left?"

"Not right away. I sat there for a while wondering what I should do—how long I should wait. I got out and checked the door, but it was locked. There were no lights in the office window upstairs. I looked for another door, but that was the only one."

"When did you leave?"

"I finally gave up around quarter to ten. Got back in the car and drove home. I was going to call him up the other day to find out where he got to but then all hell broke loose and it slipped my mind. I still don't know why he wasn't there. And I guess my alibi is in the dumpster right now."

"I'll have my work cut out for me, but don't give up hope. We've got to get a break somewhere. Hopefully it will come soon."

Jack wasn't at all sure what sort of break he was looking for. Anything would be good at this point. How about someone just showing up and saying, "I was there. I saw him. He's the guy who was in the parking lot at the SuperSave warehouse."

Isn't going to happen. Stinker, he thought

Brendan was going to spend at least one evening in the city lockup. That much was sure. Jack would have to hustle to track down some solid evidence to confirm his alibi. And hopefully, someone would claim Jane Doe as their daughter or sister, or something. Maybe the cops would discover the motive for the murder along with the perpetrator. And where did the weapon go? There was a knife somewhere with that girl's blood on it. Hopefully, there was a fingerprint or two belonging to the animal that last held it. And clothes. The perpetrator couldn't get away without getting the girl's blood on them.

The sun was low in the sky when Jack finally pulled into the parking lot of the SuperSave Groceries warehouse.

Refrigerator trucks idled by the loading dock, waiting their turn to disgorge their freight. Smaller vehicles, bearing the green and red logo of the SuperSave chain, were parked for the night. Early in the morning, they would head out to the supermarkets to provide fresh stock for the shelves.

On the loading dock, green-clad men and women with

dollies or forklifts moved back and forth with boxes and pallets of SuperSave's stock.

Jack found a spot in the visitors' lot and stepped out onto the asphalt. He surveyed the scene and made a mental note of the set-up of the compound. As he looked, what caught his eye made his heart race. He knew immediately he would have a question and perhaps a big favor to ask of Garry Forbes.

When he arrived at the visitors' desk in the upstairs office, he knew he would have to wait a while longer to hear the man's explanation for not meeting Brendan. The receptionist was in the midst of closing for the day and informed him that there was no one who could help him right now. Could he come back in the morning? They opened at eight.

Jack thanked her, and trudged back downstairs to his car. If he could get what he wanted from Forbes, at least Brendan might go free. This was assuming, of course, that he had been telling the truth. For tonight, anyway, his friend was being housed at the expense of the city. Nothing else could be done. But there was, at least, a glimmer of hope.

That evening, Jack made notes and planned his movements for the next day. He would be up early, though he knew he would have to force himself from a warm bed. The activities of the past couple of days were beginning to wear him down.

The clock radio was turned to face the bed on this particular night. He slept fitfully and with one eye watched the illuminated face, waiting for the hour to come.

Jack was startled awake at seven-thirty by the weather report from the local radio station. He washed and dressed.

After what he judged to be a truly dreadful cup of instant coffee and a granola bar, he headed out to the industrial park again to look for Garry Forbes at SuperSave Groceries. If all went as Jack hoped it would, he would come away from the meeting with fairly substantial evidence of Brendan's innocence or guilt. It could go either way.

The industrial park had grown up to the west of the city. It had once been an older, rundown residential area but in recent years new developments had been established. The trip was not quite as unpleasant as it once might have been. The district now housed families who worked in the city to the east. The drive went quickly for Jack. He pitied those headed in the opposite direction. The morning commuter traffic clogged the roads and it looked as if everything was on the verge of a standstill.

Jack pulled into the SuperSave compound a little after eight and went directly to the office. He spoke to the receptionist.

"Yes. Mr. Forbes is in. May I tell him your name? He's on the phone at the moment, but will be able to see you as soon as he's free. Would he like a cookie while he waited?

"They're our own brand," the receptionist continued. "We have them made to our own specifications with only natural ingredients. I think you'll find them to be equal to the best you have ever had."

The youngish-looking woman at the counter had a broad smile, and a plate full of SuperSavoury Chocolate Chip Delight cookies. Jack asked himself why they didn't just put this woman in front of a camera and let her do her morning greeting to visitors. Surely she would sell a boatload of their product.

The receptionist busied herself with other duties, but returned now and then to make sure Jack was getting the minimum daily requirement of SuperSavoury Chocolate Chip Delight cookies and coffee. He was easy to convince.

Garry Forbes was a tall man. Over six feet, Jack guessed. He looked fit. The kind of man who probably went running on his lunch break. If he were eating the company wares, he'd likely need the exercise. He appeared to be in his early thirties, with a mustache and a goatee. He wore office casual—dress pants and long-sleeved blue shirt, but no tie. His phone call had ended, and he had come to the reception desk where he was introduced to Jack.

"Let's go to my office. What can I help you with today?"

Jack waited to be inside with the door shut before going into the details of his mission. There was no doubt that Forbes was the right man for the job of promoting the company and its products. If Jack had been a potential customer, he would have been ready to buy. He was going to have to get in a supply of cookies. That was sure.

Forbes sat easily in his office chair, his left arm resting on the desk. Jack was offered a chair to one side.

"How can I help you, Mr. Elton? I understand this has something to do with Brendan Biggs. I heard, on the news, that he's in some sort of trouble."

Jack explained about the body in the office. Forbes had heard most of this, he knew, but the man listened attentively nonetheless, paying close attention to what the private investigator was saying.

"Apparently, you had an appointment with Mr. Biggs on the evening of the murder. He says he came here to meet you and to discuss an advertising contract with his firm. He says you never showed up."

For the first time since they had met, Forbes' face fell noticeably. He reached across his desk, and opened a date book. Jack steeled himself to hear that there had been no meeting planned, and that Biggs must have been mistaken. His alibi was about to go down the drain and he wouldn't need Jack as much as he would need a really good lawyer.

"Oh no! This is awful, Mr. Elton. I'm so sorry. What can I say?"

"Call me Jack, Mr. Forbes. Just tell me. I'm ready for it."

"Please. Call me Garry. No, Jack it's not what you think. I'm feeling just so foolish. I don't know what I was thinking. I did have an appointment with Brendan. We were going to meet here just after nine. My son had basketball that night, and I had to pick him up at the school." He pointed to the page in his diary where the appointment was written in black ink.

"But you didn't keep the appointment."

"The game went on longer than usual. I wasn't thinking, I guess. We had had a busy day here. The appointment must have slipped my mind. As you can see, I wrote it in my personal diary. But, the girls out front, who would normally remind me, didn't have it in their appointment book. It was after hours, and . . . I guess I didn't tell them."

He continued. "I picked up my son, took him home, and then went to bed. I am so sorry if my failure has caused Mr. Biggs all this trouble."

Jack brightened.

"That certainly would explain why the police were told you had no appointments that evening."

Keegan Willis had taken great pleasure in sharing this tidbit when Jack had called to verify some details about the investigation with Ted Brown. The detective happened to have been out of the office, at the time.

"Well, all may not be lost, Garry. I wonder if you can help me. I need something from you."

"I'll certainly do whatever I can. What do you need?"

Chapter Eleven

Half an hour later, his meeting ended, and Jack was headed back to police headquarters. He hoped he could press his case with Detectives Brown and Willis.

True to his word, Garry Forbes had done all he could. A small box sat on the seat beside Jack—a gift for the condemned man—from his friend at SuperSave Groceries. More than a gift. It could prove to be Brendan's ticket out of prison. Jack wondered if it would be enough.

It all sounded so easy when it was rattling around in his head and when he was in control of what happened in his imagination. Jack wondered if it would all play out so easily once he was back downtown, and trying to make it happen in reality.

Getting Brendan out of jail was not going to be enough. This was becoming an obsession with Jack. He knew the police would sort things out eventually, but this dead girl was waking him up at night with questions he couldn't answer.

Jack drove into the visitors' parking lot and parked.

"That guy sure looks like a criminal to me. Look at the

way he's skulking around, peering in the windows, and rattling the door. I'd arrest him on the spot, if I had the power to do it."

"Aw, Jack, cut it out. Don't you think I've suffered enough? I want out of here. Take this to Brown and his buddy and tell them to let me go." Brendan looked mildly amused at his friend's attempt at levity, but his voice betrayed his frustration with his present circumstances.

Jack had been able to get the use of a small office with a monitor and a video tape player. On the screen was the image of a building at night. These were pictures from a high definition security camera. A lone vehicle could be seen driving into the parking lot, which was empty except for some delivery trucks parked in the distance.

For a time there was no activity evident on the screen. After ten minutes or so, the driver got out of his car. He looked around the empty lot and approached the building. He peered into a couple of ground floor windows and then looked up to the second floor. He walked to the door and tried to open it. It appeared to be locked. The man gave a frustrated shrug and then headed back to his car. Before he got back in, he looked in the direction of the camera. At the bottom of the screen, a counter read "21:36:22 SSGC," followed by the date. The events on the tape had been recorded at thirty-six minutes past nine, the evening of the murder. The camera belonged to SSGC—SuperSave Groceries Company. The image was from the parking lot of the warehouse. The visitors' entrance was clearly visible. Jack hit the pause button. The features of the man were very familiar. There was no doubt. It was the face of Brendan Biggs.

"Well, we know where you were the evening of the murder. I think we can get you out of here—eventually. I can at least start the ball rolling. It will depend on whether they have some other reason to keep you, and just how much more paperwork they want to generate."

"I told them where I was. They didn't believe me. Now they have proof." Brendan's frustration was giving way to elation. Perhaps he was jumping the gun.

"Yeah, well, the wheels of justice grind fairly slow these days. Make yourself comfortable. Don't make any plans till you are out the main entrance of this place."

"Thanks, I'll keep that in mind," Brendan said, looking crestfallen again.

Jack stood up, went to the door and signaled the uniformed officer who stood with a bored expression on his face, in the hallway. The cop pulled out a ring of keys on the end of a retractable line attached to his belt. He unlocked the door.

Jack waited with Brendan while another officer was called to escort him back to his cell. He ejected the tape Forbes had got for him and went looking for Chief Detective Brown.

Brown and Willis were in the office, and heading for the door, when Jack finally caught up with them.

"Morning guys. Got a minute?" Keegan Willis looked ready to say 'no' but deferred to his superior.

"What have you got on your mind, Elton?" Brown asked. He stopped his forward progress and looked at Jack with genuine interest.

"I've got a question and some evidence for you. I'd appreciate it if you could give me a little of your time."

The three stepped into an empty interrogation room and sat around the table. Ordinarily, it was the police asking the questions in this room. The irony was not lost on Jack.

Keegan Willis had the look of a man with more important things to do. He sat, elbows on the table, combing his hair with the fingers of his right hand. The fingers of his left hand drummed on the tabletop.

"What have you got for us?" Willis asked.

"Wait a second, officer. I've got a question first." Jack asked about the quick arrest and the slim evidence.

Brown would be the spokesman for the police department.

"You're right. We initially only had Biggs' lack of an alibi to go on. Then we discovered a note on the victim, with his name and a time written on it. We kept it from the press and other interested parties, like you, because we needed to check things out. We had hoped to get an ID on our girl before now, so we could check out some other leads. You know—friends, family, business associates. Like that."

"You mean to say this girl had Brendan's name on a note, and you're using that as your reason to hold him here?" Jack's voice was considerably higher in pitch than usual.

"We had a victim in an office owned by the man whose name was on the paper. The time, written on the paper was nine-thirty; the time we figure she was likely being killed. He can't prove he wasn't there. We need to interrogate him, and he is an obvious flight risk. We brought him in. It's only been about a day, so far. We're looking for clues. That's all I can tell you."

"Have you found the murder weapon?"

"Nothing yet. Coroner figures a knife like one of those fancy, folding, hunting blades. It left telltale markings that put it in a particular class. So far, no knife, and therefore no fingerprints, at least nothing that matches any in the database."

"Sure wish they had been a little more careful to preserve the crime scene before we arrived that morning," Willis said, with a look of disgust on his face. "There were fingerprints all over the place. We collected what we could. We may never find anything we can use."

"How about I give you an alibi for your chief suspect?" Jack held up the surveillance tape.

Willis' eyebrows performed a face-lifting maneuver at the sight of the cassette. Brown reached out and took the tape from Jack's outstretched hand.

"Let's have a look." He went to a trolley holding a monitor and video machine, and pressed the tape to the mechanical mouth. The device sucked in the black plastic case, and the monitor screen went blue momentarily. Shortly, the picture fluttered and the image of the SuperSave parking lot was displayed.

The black Jaguar belonging to Brendan Biggs pulled into the visitor's space, and the same short drama Jack had viewed with his friend was played out, just as before.

When it was all over, the chief detective made the machine regurgitate the tape, and placed it on the table.

Turning to his assistant, Ted Brown asked, in what Jack considered to be a reasonably level voice for a man who had just been shown evidence that his department should have acquired first, "Keegan, how come we have to wait for Jack to bring us this? What were you doing when you were down there, supposedly interviewing people? First you miss the fact that there was an appointment scheduled. Now, it seems, there was visual evidence supporting the alibi of the guy you were so certain was our perpetrator."

As the questions hung in the air, Jack was pleased by the look that had appeared on Keegan Willis' face.

"I'll have to run this by a few more people first," Brown said to Jack, "but I think you can safely assume that Biggs will be able to go home soon. Just how soon, I can't say."

"I'm sure he'll be very happy to hear that." Jack smiled at

the officers. "I'll just leave that tape with you. I'll take it back to SuperSave when you don't need it any more."

"I think we might take it back, Jack," Brown said. "We'd like to get some confirmation from the folks there. I assume this is a copy of the master tape."

Before he left the building, Jack discovered that there was a plan to get pictures of the dead woman to the papers and TV that afternoon. The grisly truth was that, lacking any other means, they had had a photo taken of the girl in the morgue. There was only so much touching up they could do to hide the ravages of death and the progress of decay. This would be the image that people would see on the six o'clock news, and on the front of their morning papers the next day. Hopefully the response would be reasonably quick, and the picture could be retired. Jack hoped that a family member, or a friend, might have a happier, healthier looking representation of the victim.

Chapter Twelve

Jack hadn't been able to give much thought to Valerie lately. That was not a good sign. Valerie was someone who deserved being thought of—often.

Their schedules, lately, had not allowed them to spend time together. Valerie's job, as a peace officer, did not allow much free time, and recent events had kept Jack's mind on other things. The situation was bad indeed, Jack thought, when he couldn't find time to think about the most beautiful girl in the world.

Valerie was at work when Jack called from a pay phone, a few blocks from the police station. His dislike of cell phones wavered, at times like this, when he considered the convenience of not having to drive around the city, looking for a place to park, close to a phone booth. Sometimes, without thinking, he would feed a parking meter only to realize too late that he had given it the coins he needed for the call.

"How's it going?" he had asked.

"Same old, same old," had been her reply. "I'm getting abused, just like always. I can't get no respect. What's up?"

"I need an ear. Got a moment?"

"I think so. My buddy is taking care of someone in a hurry, who will now be late, and a few bucks poorer, if you catch my drift. I'm minding the store, so to speak. If I have to leave in a hurry, I hope you'll understand."

"Making more big bucks for the city, eh? Anyway, here's the thing. I got this dead girl."

"With you?" she asked, in mock surprise.

"Very funny. You know that girl that was found dead in an office downtown, two or three nights ago?"

"Okay. I remember that."

"They found a note on her that says she was supposed to meet a friend of mine. Guy who owns the office."

"I'd say that was incriminating evidence," Val replied.

"But, get this. My friend, Brendan, wasn't there. He has an alibi. He swears he's never met her."

"Bummer."

"Yeah. And I can't figure out why she would have a note like that."

"Seems to me, you need to find out who wrote the note," Val said. "That could be difficult. Then you need to find out where the info came from, and why she had, or thought she had, an appointment."

"She's not talking," Jack said as he ran his hand through his hair in frustration. He stood shaking his head. Around him, traffic and pedestrians passed back and forth, unaware of his dilemma.

"Someone's gotta talk," Val said. "Look, I gotta go right now. My buddy needs me. Call me when I'm not working. Good luck."

"Thanks." The line had gone dead.

Jack hung up. He waited to hear the sound of his money dropping into the collection box but ran his finger through the coin return, just in case.

Val had an analytical mind. It was good to get her take on these things, even if only to confirm the obvious. Less and less was clear to Jack as the case progressed.

As he drove through lunch hour traffic, Jack reflected some more on the meaning of the note.

Brendan swore he had never met her. Who wrote the note? Did she? Did someone else? Did they copy the name from the phone book, or was it given over the phone? Maybe it was given to her in person.

The girl didn't look like your average advertising client. She did not have the appearance of an artist looking for a job. But then Jack told himself he wouldn't really know what a production artist would look like.

Jack headed for the offices of Western Express Cleaning. They were the folks who were under contract to Biggs, Wilberforce, Hutton, and Small, for janitorial services at the eleventh floor office. He wanted to talk to their man, and ask if he had seen anything unusual on that night when the girl had an appointment to die.

A boxy-looking warehouse sat at the end of a row of industrial buildings in an older part of the city. Though a few new-looking vans proclaimed their association with Western Express Cleaning, the building that also carried the name had seen better times. Old metal siding had been painted blue some time in the last century. A once-white door now displayed the gray and black hand prints of a number of eager workers who had pushed that portal open over the years. Grass grew up around the cracked cement walkway leading to the soiled door. It was a good thing that prospective clients could depend on a visit at their places of business to sign their cleaning contracts. If they ever came here they might think twice, in spite of the sparkling appearance of the company vehicles.

Jack parked by the curb and made his way up the cracked walkway. The doorknob rattled loosely as he made his way into a small office, with an antique appearance to match what he had seen outside. The place smelled of cleaning fluid and cigar smoke. Behind the counter, in dirty coveralls was the source of the cigar smoke and some other unsavory odors that increased in intensity with proximity.

"Yeah bud, can I help you?" the cigar asked.

Jack wondered if Brendan knew about these corporate offices and if he would still want to use their services if he ever visited them.

"I'm looking for someone who can help me find one of your employees. I'm looking for a man who serviced the offices of Biggs, Wilberforce, Hutton, and Small, recently."

"You got some kind of complaint, mister? Ya gotta fill out a written report for that. We don't give no refunds till we got both sides o' the story. We may not be pretty, but we try to do a good job."

"Hey, hang on there. I'm sure there are no complaints," Jack said. "I'm investigating a murder that took place over there, and I'm wondering if your man can help."

"I heard about that. Cops were here. Terrible thing, that girl getting killed, and all. Can't help you. We were told not to come."

"No, I don't mean the day after the murder. I'm talking about the night before."

The cigar beckoned Jack closer to the counter with a nicotine-stained finger.

"Like I told the cops, we were called off two nights in a row. The guys around here were saying it was a good thing we hadn't been there that night. One of us might have been killed ourselves. No, sir. We were not there. I can show you in the log book."

"But one of your men, an older fellow, was there that night. A new employee or part-time, perhaps? Can you tell me where to find him? Maybe he went there by mistake."

"Wouldn't happen."

"Why not?"

"First off, we never send just one guy over there. There is too much to be done. Besides, the guy would kill himself lugging equipment up and down from the truck. I've been there. We need the big floor polisher for the reception area. Then there's the carpet steamer. They like to have the carpets real clean. We got our shampooer for the boss' office and a wagonload of cleaning supplies to clean stuff and supply the washrooms. One guy just couldn't handle it."

"And the other thing?"

"We don't have any seniors working for us. Not that we wouldn't hire them, if they was qualified. We just don't have any. You're going to have to look somewhere else."

This was not the way Jack had envisioned his encounter unfolding. The mystery was not supposed to deepen. He needed answers. He could see he was going to have to make another late night visit to the security desk.

"One last thing," Jack said.

"Wassat?" the cigar asked.

"What did the police say, when they found out you'd been called off two nights in a row?"

"To tell you the truth, Mack, one of the guys looked kinda pleased to hear that. Said something about it proving some guy they suspected had planned the murder."

Jack thanked the man, and headed back outside, into the fresh air. He walked toward his car flapping his jacket in the hope of getting rid of the smell before he had to drive in the enclosed space. He was only mildly successful in that task.

Jack was beginning to wonder whether he hadn't bitten off a little more than he could chew. He seemed no closer to getting the answers that would solve this riddle than he had been the first day. He hoped that something would come along, to at least open the door a crack, so that he could make a beginning at seeking the solution.

He wished, too, that he hadn't shunned modern technology quite so readily. A cell phone would have been handy right about now, as he worked his way through traffic. He could find out if Brendan was still at police headquarters. He could call the security company to find out if the guard he had spoken to would be working again tonight. More importantly, he could call ahead and have a pizza made up, so that he wouldn't have to wait for it. He had missed lunch. He was hungry.

Jack found a little restaurant that advertised The Best Pizza Anywhere. While he was waiting, he fed coins to a pay phone that felt like it had been coated in cooking oil. He tried to keep it away from his mouth and prevent the receiver from pressing against his ear.

Screaming coming from the restaurant's kitchen, in a language he did not understand, made it hard to hear anyone on the other end of the line.

When he called the advertising office, the number was

busy. *Must be doing a lot of business today,* he thought as he hung up and tried the number of the police department.

This time the phone was answered on the first ring. The argument in the kitchen had subsided enough for him to be able to communicate. When he made his request, he was put through to an officer who informed him that Mr. Biggs was still there, but that he had seen paperwork indicating that Brendan would be back on the street soon. Yes, Mr. Elton was welcome to come and wait for the process to finish, so he could take Mr. Biggs home. He might have to be patient, though. The clerks were busy and they needed a signature from Detective Brown. He wasn't there at the moment.

Jack made one last call to inquire about the night guard at Biggs, Wilberforce, Hutton, and Small. He was asked to hold on the first ring. For the next five minutes he was entertained by tinny music from a radio station that was apparently wired to the phone system.

He was urged to buy a new car, use a revolutionary detergent. The weather was sunny with a sixty percent chance of rain. "Sports will be coming up next, after this word . . ."

The line clicked and Jack was asked how the security company might be of assistance. He asked his question and, after another pause for a musical interlude, a polite young female voice informed him that Graham was scheduled to begin his shift at the regular time that evening. Jack thanked the voice and hung up.

Back in the restaurant, a square box with his name on it sat by the cash register. He gazed into his empty wallet and then looked for some indication that the eatery accepted plastic. He handed over his card and after the necessary procedures was given the box, the receipt, and his VISA.

In the car, Jack opened the box and took out a slice of his

pizza 'all-dressed.' One bite told him he was eating The Best Pizza Anywhere—within ten feet of the sign on the restaurant. He closed the box and left it beside him on the passenger seat. For now, one slice was more than enough. He would need to be a whole lot more hungry before he went in there again.

Police headquarters was getting to be a terribly familiar place. Same route. Same parking spot. Same office. *I've got to stop doing this,* he reminded himself, as he was passed through the door yet again. He was informed that it would not be possible to see Mr. Biggs in the cells right now. Apparently someone was being booked and, for security reasons, civilians were not permitted in that area of the building while prisoners were being locked in.

"Okay, I'll wait," Jack said to the officer at the desk. The young man gave him a strange look, and returned to his paperwork.

What a dumb thing to say, Jack thought to himself. *Of course you'll wait, jackass. You don't have another option. The cop just told you that.*

He went to the waiting room that had been indicated to him, and sat in one of the plastic chairs along the wall. These things could not have been designed for regular people, with normal posture. If he leaned back a little too far, he could feel himself sliding forward on the seat. That part of the chair seemed shorter than necessary so that he was in danger of having his behind disappear over the edge of the seat and ending up sitting on the floor. The only position that seemed to work was a sort of hunched-over Rodin's *The Thinker* pose, with his elbows resting on his knees. Some design professional had left a gaping hole at the back of the chair so that his butt hung out the back, like one of those baboons at the zoo. He was glad he didn't have any company at this particular point in the investigation. This was just another reason to hope the police would spring Brendan soon.

While he waited, Jack looked through some of the antique magazines lying on a low table in the middle of the room. "There's probably something in here announcing the launch of the Titanic," he muttered to himself.

After what seemed like hours, Jack was informed that Brendan Biggs would be up in a moment and would be free to go. He could pick him up in the lobby.

Jack asked the whereabouts of the two detectives and was told they were in the department office. He arranged for Brendan to be given a message to wait for him and, after getting the necessary clearance, went in search of the officers.

"I see your friend is out, for now," Keegan Willis said, as he looked up from his desk. "Tell him not to leave town any time soon."

"That's your job officer. And I'm sure you've already informed him of his obligation to keep himself available. Where's Brown?"

The young officer motioned with his head to indicate his boss across the room by the bulletin board.

Jack threaded his way between the desks of the other officers and came up alongside the chief detective. He stood for a moment, looking at the poster the officer had just tacked to the wall.

"Not the most flattering picture, is it?" Jack asked.

"Best we could do under the circumstances. Dead people always tend to look lifeless in all their photos postmortem.

It's a job getting them to smile. But they do keep really still for their close-ups. I just hope someone knows her and gets in touch with us."

Graveyard humor, Jack thought. *The police officer's defense against going completely mad in the midst of all this insanity.*

"It would be nice to get some more information about her," Jack said. "Right now everything we think we know is only conjecture. You guys really have your work cut out for you."

"It's not the first case to leave us baffled for awhile, as you well know, but we'll get it sorted out eventually. No matter how good or bad you are, someone's going to remember you. You can't remain anonymous forever."

"No, but sometimes you can remain anonymous for a very long time."

"We'll just have to hope that this isn't one of those times."

Jack left the detectives and headed out to the reception area to find his friend. Eventually, Brendan was brought out by a uniformed officer through the same electronically controlled door Jack had used to get in. He was unshaven, and looked like he needed a week's sleep. He smelled like he could have used a shower.

"So, how did you enjoy the city's hospitality?" Jack asked, smiling.

"Sort of a minimalist decor. The bed was a little hard. The food was a little blander than I'm used to. The neighbors kept looking in. But the security system can't be beat."

The two men walked out into the early evening and headed for Jack's car. Brendan gave the vehicle a distressed look. "I guess it's no worse than what I just came from."

"Here, have some of this. It's The Best Pizza Anywhere." Jack had to control himself to keep from laughing as he steered the car out of the parking lot.

"Hey, this is good," said Brendan as he dug another piece out of the box.

Jack shook his head in disbelief and thought to himself, *There's one thing money can't buy, and that's a good set of working taste buds.*

Chapter Thirteen

A short while later, Jack and Brendan pulled up to the office tower housing Biggs, Wilberforce, Hutton, and Small. The trip across town had been relatively uneventful. Brendan had not said much, except to express his thanks to his friend for sticking with him, and taking care of his interests.

"So, what are you going to do now?" Jack asked.

"First off, I'm getting out of these clothes. Then I'm going to take a very long bath. I may just sleep through tomorrow. Then I guess I'll have to get caught up with the work that I've missed, and maybe have a heart-to-heart with the staff. They just may have a question or two. It's been tough on all of us. Some of them may take a while to recover, myself included. How about you?"

"This whole thing has got me tied in knots, trying to figure out what happened up there."

Jack looked out his window and up the front of the building. He turned back to his friend.

"I've got to get some answers. To do that, I'm going to have

104

to ask some questions. You should know that someone called off your janitorial service the night our girl was murdered."

Brendan's eyes grew several sizes. "You mean someone planned this all to happen in my office? That's . . . that's pre-meditated murder."

"That's what it sounds like. It means there was a reason that girl was killed. Someone carefully orchestrated this, from what I can tell. Why, I don't know."

"How did they know I would be out of the office by then?"

"I don't know. Near as I can figure, they weren't counting on you being there at all. I think they were counting on you keeping office hours. Just expected the office to be empty. You were lucky. You could have ended up dead on the floor beside the girl."

"Whoa! Wouldn't that have made for a front-page story? Why my office?"

"I don't know that yet. Don't know if I ever will. I'll have to keep you posted."

"Are there any suspects? I mean, apart from present company."

"No one to put a name to, but maybe we have a chance to track down our suspect. I've got to talk to your security guy tonight."

"Jeez, I appreciate your dedication."

"I guess it's the cop still in me. We'll see whether this leads anywhere. Besides, this mystery keeps me awake nights." Jack smiled. "Might as well use my insomnia creatively. And while I'm on the topic of security . . ."

"Go on," Brendan replied.

"Next time you've got some money for upgrades, for goodness sake, get a security camera for the office."

Brendan opened the passenger side door and slid out of

the car. "I'll remember that," he said, as he tossed the empty pizza box onto the back seat. "Thanks for supper. I owe you one," he added, wiping his face with his hand before closing the door.

Jack watched Brendan fishing in his pocket for keys, as he walked toward the outdoor parking lot. He pulled away from the curb when he saw that his friend was safely inside the Jaguar. It was too early to interrogate Graham, the night watchman. Jack still felt as if he hadn't eaten all day. Brendan's hunger had been satisfied. But Jack wanted real food.

He drove into Chinatown, and managed to find a place to park. This city was famous for the oriental enclave that sat squarely in the midst of the business district.

The entrance to the area was marked by a tall, gold leaf-encrusted gateway. Its bright colors and imposing size made it hard to miss. Behind this portal lay a place of history. Here, in the days when the country was just being settled, Chinese and Japanese immigrants came to live. They worked hard, and received little appreciation for their efforts.

Some had built the railway. Others had farmed the land. Some of the older citizens could recount the history surrounding their coming to a new country. Part of the story involved intolerance, and prejudice, and mistrust. It was a history that Jack knew very little about.

There was mystery here too. There were the tales of the opium trade, in the days when the drug was legal, and the years that followed, when it was not. If one looked carefully, or had a willing guide, they could still find small doors in narrow alleys that used to lead to secret and mysterious places. They did that no more, as far as Jack could tell.

Now the mystery resided in the people and their traditions. It was a different kind of community. For all the years of its existence in the midst of western culture, the people who lived here, at least, kept much to themselves. They were a proud people who honored tradition and held their elders in proper esteem. Respect and honor were highly valued. Family was important. Community was equally so.

Jack had to admit that there was also a subculture, small though it appeared, that engaged in activities that were frowned upon by East and West alike. He wondered if the death of the girl was related to something illegal, some debt that had to be paid. It was a possibility that had to be considered.

Liang Bamboo Garden had a Chinese buffet that would satisfy even the most discriminating diner. It was here that Jack decided to spend the early evening. Here, he knew, he could learn to forget the unfortunate meal of the early afternoon.

He took a heaping plate to a corner table and satiated himself with the flavors of the orient, mixed liberally with food called 'Chinese' that had been created for the western palate. As he ate, he watched people come and go. He observed different little groups and noted what they ate. And he thought about the girl.

Over by a window was a young western family with their children—a boy of about four and a girl, probably six. Mom and dad were eating chop suey and chow mein dishes. Each had an egg roll and a meat dish. The two kids were eating all the fried things—chicken balls, shrimp, won-tons—covered with a thick red sauce so it was almost impossible to tell what lay beneath.

Partway through his meal, he observed a young Chinese man enter with two raven-haired beauties, who looked like they straddled both cultures. They laughed and talked, in English. It was the conversation of college students. Jack couldn't hear all that was said, but it was clear they enjoyed each other's company. He wondered if they were celebrating the end of exams or perhaps using this evening as an excuse not to study.

An older couple sat in an area almost hidden from the rest of the diners. They were very quiet. The old man was demonstrating great care, and giving undivided attention to his wife. She sat smiling, enjoying the time together. Jack noticed that the serving staff was giving them the measure of respect that should be shown honored members of the community. He saw, too, that they were not eating like everyone else. Not only were they using chopsticks with amazing dexterity—Jack marveled at how they ate rice with the bamboo utensils—but they were eating completely different food from everyone else. They did not visit the buffet. They had not been shown a menu. They had spoken quietly to their server and he had hurried off, without writing anything down, having bowed deeply to them both. Jack thought to himself that whatever it was they had been served, it was likely a true Chinese dish, not the fried up bits of chicken, beef and fish that was served to westerners who didn't know any better.

He watched all this while he ate the unauthenticated components of his meal and sipped endless small cups of a particularly flavorful green tea. And he continued to wonder about the girl.

The sky was completely dark by the time Jack finished his meal. He paid his bill, and stuffed the credit card receipt in his pants pocket, where it would likely be laundered sometime soon. He stepped out onto the street and headed back to his car.

Though the sun had set, the street was as bright as day.

The lights of the buildings combined with the streetlights made this part of town glow, like a jewel, in the darkness. Gold and silver mixed with red and green, to give the scene a festive air even when it wasn't a time of special celebration. Jack would have to come back again, he knew. The next time might not be quite as satisfying, or nearly as restful. He unlocked the car and got in. He turned the key and looked out on the sight that spread before him.

Maybe the answer is out there, on this street, he thought to himself before heading to the dark office tower.

As he approached the building, he could see through the window that Graham was already in his place, feet up on the desk, fighting sleep, ever on guard for the folks who depended on his alertness at this time of night.

Jack pressed close to the window and tapped on the glass. The night watchman's head shot up and at the sight of a familiar face, he smiled, unfolded himself from his perch, and slowly crossed the concourse to the locked lobby door.

"Well, hi again," he said as Jack entered. Then, "What are you doing back here tonight?" over his shoulder as he hurried back to his chair.

"I've got a few more questions for you and I need you to give some thought to what exactly you saw the night of the murder. Do you think you might be able to do that for me?"

"Sure. Why not? I've got a little time on my hands here." Graham smiled.

"I want you to try to remember exactly what went on that night. It is very important that you tell me who you remember coming and going. Did you see people come that you did not see leave? Was there anyone who left that you don't remember signing in? Anyone unusual?"

"Wow! That's a lot of questions. I gotta think a little. Besides, we talked about all this stuff a few days ago, didn't we?"

"Yes, we did. But I need you to think about it again. Maybe there was something you missed the first time. If you can think of anything at all, it could make a difference in solving the case."

Graham lifted his cap and scratched his head. Then he replaced the headgear and stared off into the distance. He was quiet for a long time. Jack thought he might have drifted off to sleep. Then the guard spoke.

"I came in at my regular time, just before eight, and relieved Scrivens. He didn't report anything unusual. You can always scan the book again, if you want to see the activity log. Security is a little more rigid around here. Lots of stuff on the upper floors that needs protecting, I guess. At night, the elevator always stops at this floor on the way up. I see anyone in there and they've gotta check in.

"That night the only one who didn't check in was Mr. Biggs. He was already here. He's signed in on the morning activity log. He got down here after nine that night and was looking a little stressed. He went out and I didn't see him come back during my shift."

"Could he have come in without your seeing him?" Jack asked.

"Like I said before, I think he's got a pass key to the door. He's also got a key for the elevator so he can override the controls and shoot right to the eleventh floor. If he came in the front door, he could have gone back up without my seeing him when I was doing my rounds. But I was here till four in the morning, when the shift changed and the elevator did not move after eleven o'clock. That's when the cleaning staff usually leaves for the night from Biggs' place. I didn't see it. I just know that's when they usually leave."

"So you are still sure you did not see the cleaning guy leave that night?"

"I'd remember. Like I said, he was new. I'd remember a stranger leaving, I think."

"Tell me everything you remember about this guy."

"Well, he came in about . . ." Graham's eyes glazed a little as he stared into the distance again, focusing, Jack assumed, on an imaginary clock that had stopped at the exact time the janitor had arrived.

"He came in a little after nine-thirty, I figure. It was shortly before I was scheduled to do my walk around."

"Describe the man for me." Jack leaned closer.

"Older than me, definitely. Shorter than me. Maybe five-foot-five, or six. Wore a baseball cap. Thinning hair. I saw it when he lifted his cap to scratch his head. Sorta salt and pepper color. Looked older than the guys we usually get. Maybe late fifties. He didn't strike me as the sort of guy that they usually hire. I didn't think he was capable of handling the equipment. Come to think of it, when I saw him, he didn't have any equipment. I mentioned that last time, I think."

"How was he dressed?"

"Like usual. Kind of a gray uniform. Had the name 'Frank' on the pocket. Funny thing, though. Usually the back of the thing says 'Western Express' but he didn't have anything on his."

"Did you talk to him?"

"Not much. He didn't have a lot to say. Just 'hello' and 'good-bye.' Besides, he didn't talk very loud. Signed the book and was on his way up to the office."

"Think carefully. Did you see anyone else that night? Anyone you had not seen before. Perhaps someone who didn't belong."

"Well, of course, there was that woman," Graham said.

The hair on the back of Jack's neck stood to attention. "What woman?"

His tone, and the look on his face, must have startled the security guard. Graham recoiled at the question, as if he had been struck in the chest.

"Why, the woman who came looking for Mr. Biggs. She had a note saying she was to meet him. Had the room number and all."

"When did she come in? Why didn't you mention her before?" Jack was almost yelling, now.

"She came in just after Biggs left. And you didn't ask."

"What do you mean, I didn't ask?" Frustration was rising in Jack's demeanor.

"Well you were asking about folks that didn't belong. She had an appointment. I supposed she had a reason to be here. Biggs is always working late."

"Did she sign the book?"

"Jeez, I don't really know. Wanna look?"

Did he want to look? This guy had the brains of a box of rocks.

"I think that might be a really good idea." Jack was exercising all his strength to keep calm.

The guard thumbed through the logbook looking for the appropriate date. "Yeah, here it is. She came in at nine thirty-seven and went to the eleventh. Just used her initials, though. RF."

"Don't you check these things?" Jack's exasperation was showing. "Don't you check the names?"

Graham's face hardened.

"Mister, we get a whole lot of people coming and going around here. If they look like they belong, we don't pay much notice."

"Yeah, but at nine-thirty? After most people are gone? You want me to believe you are so busy sitting here that you can't make sure people leave a decent record of their visit?"

Jack could feel heat rising above his collar.

Graham just gave a shrug, as if the question wasn't that important, and added, "Maybe I shoulda kept the door locked when you came in here with all your questions. I got stuff to do."

Jack had his answer. Best to move on with the interrogation.

"You said Mr. Biggs had already left."

"Yeah, but she had an appointment. I figured he was coming back."

"But you say you never saw him come back."

"Well, yeah, but like I said, he has his own key."

Jack sighed in exasperation. "So she came in after the cleaning guy."

Graham's finger traced the page again. "Well look at this. I'll be darned. No, she came in before him. He wasn't signed in until nine-forty. He went up after she did."

"I wish I'd known this before. It might have helped a lot. I've got some more work to do, by the looks of things. I guess I'm through for tonight. If you think of anything else—anyone else—give me a call right away."

Jack wrote his number on a note pad and tore off the sheet. He offered it to the security guard who scanned it briefly before folding it and putting it into his shirt pocket.

"Always glad to help," he said.

Whole lot of help you've been so far, Jack thought. "Yeah, good," he said instead and headed for the door.

Jack drove home through a light rain wondering what criteria was used to hire folks like Graham. He was positive the requirements were higher than they appeared, and that Graham was not typical. What was the use of being observant, if what you see never gets reported, or is only mentioned during an interrogation? Maybe there was hope for Jack as a security guard if other things didn't pan out.

He parked and headed straight to his apartment. If folks had left messages on the answering machine in the office, they would still be there when he finally got around to checking them. Tonight he was tired and frustrated. His one consolation was the knowledge that Brendan Biggs was not spending another evening in the city cells. That didn't mean Jack wouldn't have to visit the police again. In fact, he was thinking that it might be a good idea to share what little information he had been able to glean from that intelligent security man, Graham, in the morning.

Tonight, though, he needed to sleep. All the running around, and probably the pizza, had left him feeling a little nauseous. Thinking had given him a headache. He made sure he couldn't see the clock radio when he finally turned out the light in his bedroom.

Chapter Fourteen

When Jack woke up, the morning sun was filtering in around the blackout curtains. The rain had stopped during the night and the day promised to be warm and cloudless.

Jack was feeling neither warm, nor cloudless. It felt like nothing had been accomplished. He knew, from experience, that the cops would be getting a little anxious for a break about now. He wished he had something more encouraging to offer.

Jack seriously doubted that Frank was the real name of the phantom office cleaner. He doubted, as well, that Frank's purpose had been to clean the office. He could only hope that the official investigation had gotten further than his un-official one. The way things were going, that was in some doubt. Each new piece of evidence seemed to raise more questions than it answered.

He drove more slowly today. It didn't feel like there was anything to be urgent about. What he had to share did not seem particularly earth-shattering, and it certainly wasn't likely to be classified as the tip that 'broke the case wide open.'

He walked, hunched over, head down, to the main doors of the police headquarters. He asked to speak to Brown and Willis. They were out. He really needed to get a cell phone. Maybe if this case paid off . . .

"Is Ron Leung around?" he asked the officer at reception.

He would put the time to good use while he waited for the two detectives to get back from their coffee break. Leung might be his ticket into a world he only knew by reputation, and from brief observation. He would pick the officer's brain for ideas and information. There would be no harm in telling him what he knew about the victim. Perhaps the Chinese detective could give him some new insights and, if Jack was lucky, formulate a motive for the murder.

Ron Leung was a good detective. He had been born right here, in the city, thirty-three years ago. His parents had emigrated from China the year before that. They had set to work, immediately, to become an asset to their new homeland.

Ron's father was a surgeon at the hospital. His mother contented herself to work at home. From the beginning they had wanted only the best for their son and had made sure that he received the best education they could afford.

Ron had attended private schools, which accounted for his North American accent, and his continued interest in staying up-to-date on all those subjects that interested him. The skills he had learned in school had served him well.

After high school, the young man had headed to college, for a degree in police sciences. His father had hoped he would head across the country to one of the universities that offered medicine, but Ron was determined to work in law enforcement.

This interest had developed in his younger years, as he watched racial profiling put some of his friends under the scrutiny of the police. Whether they had been involved in something illegal or not, those who showed Asian facial features were often singled out when the police were looking for someone on whom to pin the blame. Ron determined to turn that around by working from the inside to bring reform. And, by setting a good example, he hoped to be able to mentor other young men so they, too, might choose a profession in law. It was evident to all that Ron was succeeding in his crusade.

He had started in the city police, walking a beat in Chinatown. His presence had proved a comfort to the people there, who were always a little shy when it came to approaching officers of other ethnic backgrounds. The mistrust seemed to have cut both ways in days gone by. The hope was that some of that had changed.

Ron had an easygoing way about him that made him appear non-threatening. At the same time, he had a determined spirit that made him stick to a task until he was satisfied that the best had been done. Some of his fellow officers had nicknamed him Pit Bull because of that tenacity.

Leung's days on the beat had gone a long way toward bringing greater respect for the local police. Often, he would be chosen to serve as spokesman for the force when a bright face was needed to confront the television and press cameras. His soothing voice did much to comfort the community in times of stress.

Today, as he came to escort Jack to his office, Ron Leung looked cheerful and fit. He was close to six feet tall and slender. The man ran ten miles a day and spent three days a week in the gym.

"Can I buy you a cup of coffee?" he asked as they passed the coffee machine, on a cart in the middle of the office.

"Yes. Thanks."

"What will you have in it?" the officer asked as he poured from the glass carafe.

"Black will be fine." Jack had noticed the ever-present shaker of coffee whitener.

"So what brings you here this morning, Jack? I thought you'd had enough of this place."

"You're too kind. You know that I left under a cloud. I still have police work in my blood."

The officer gave a knowing nod, but said nothing.

Jack continued, "As far as what brings me here, I've got this puzzling case I'm dealing with, for a friend."

He went over the details of the murder with Leung. The officer continued to sit quietly, listening intently, and nodding at appropriate times to show he was still interested.

"So you see," Jack concluded, "being seen as an 'outsider,' I might have a problem talking to some of the folks who could help me most."

"The vast majority of people from that community aren't like that. A lot of the suspicion is fading. They would never knowingly mislead you, you know. But I understand what you are saying, particularly about some of the older folk who are still steeped in the tradition of their ancestors. There is always that aspect of honor that enters in, and sometimes hinders the exercise of good judgment."

"Got any ideas?"

"You could probably use some help. I might be able to spare a few hours of free time to go with you, if you need to talk to some of those folks. In some cases, you might need a translator."

"I really would appreciate that. I don't want to upset anyone, and I really want them to understand that this is for their benefit, as well as mine. I don't want a killer wandering the streets, preying on the young men and women from that part of the city—or any other part for that matter."

"Tell you what. If you get any leads that you can follow, over to Chinatown, give me a call. I'll do what I can to help. And I meant the part about a translator too. Some of the older folk still only speak their own dialect and couldn't answer your questions even if they wanted to."

"Thanks. I'll keep that in mind. Thanks for your time."

The two shook hands.

One went back to work on solving a theft at one of the city banks. The other headed out into the hustle and bustle of the main office, looking for the two detectives who shared his interest in a young woman lying dead in the morgue downstairs, and desperately in need of a name, a decent burial, and some justice.

Brown and Willis were hovering over some papers on the chief detective's desk when Jack finally found them.

He filled them in on what the security guard had revealed about the night of the crime. Jack took the liberty of expressing his opinion of the man named Graham, and his lack of sensitivity for the importance of facts.

After some serious clucking of tongues, Brown shared a little information of his own.

"These reports we were looking at, when you came in, are the result of that poster we put out, and an interview Willis here submitted to, on the evening news. It's not a big help, right now, but gives us our first few leads.

"We're got a young woman who went missing a couple days ago, named Rene Franklin. It could be our girl but we're waiting for a picture and some contact with next of kin. Initials match too.

"Mary Titus left a note for her boyfriend saying she was

leaving him. That was on Tuesday. He's bent all out of shape about it, but says the picture doesn't match. We sent a car over with a copy of the picture. The initials don't match either. That's it.

"We've got some others here. We'll follow them all up, of course, and maybe we'll see our way out of the forest before too long."

"Rene Franklin doesn't sound like a very Asian name. Where does she live?" Jack asked.

"She's over on the east side of the city. High-class stuff. That's where we keep the millionaires," Willis said.

Then Brown made a suggestion Jack thought might be helpful.

"She may have changed her name to improve her chances in business. It happens. Or, maybe only her mom is Asian. You might want to check it out. I can give you an address. We'd do it ourselves, but she seems kind of low priority, at this point, even if the initials do match. You could take the photo to the parents. I'll send an officer with you. Just remember to report back to us. I'll trust you on that."

"Thanks, I appreciate the opportunity to work with you guys again."

Jack smiled at Willis in particular. Every now and then the detective needed someone to give his chain a little tug. There was always the chance that he would change his rough exterior for something less abrasive, but Jack had known others like him who learned their approach to police work from watching TV. Willis obviously loved his cop shows.

Chapter Fifteen

J ack had never been completely clear on what had resulted in the sudden end to his police career. He knew that the consequences of his lack of judgment had been injury and pain that would keep him from engaging in the high-energy police work he had once enjoyed.

He was aware too, that lacking evidence to the contrary, he had been officially labeled as a bad cop and suspended indefinitely from the force.

What he couldn't completely figure out was why he was being given the special access he was; why other officers— even Willis—kept letting him into their world.

Officer Jack Elton had remained above reproach until the day when Sonny Lorentini had offered him a tip that, Jack had been assured, would lead to a big drug bust.

Lorentini was noted for his illegal connections, and the officer should have been more suspicious of a known criminal. The temptation to make a major arrest in the fight against narcotics trafficking was too good to resist.

Jack had gone to the house in an older part of town at the appointed time. He made the unforgivable error of going alone. When he came to, he was in the hospital with multiple fractures to his head and a broken back. When he was feeling better, he discovered that his butt was in a sling as well.

Drugs had been found in his uniform pocket. Used paraphernalia were found next to him, and a drug test indicated he had shot up recently.

Uncharacteristically, there were some individuals, already known to police, who were anxious to testify that Officer Jack Elton had gotten into a fight with his supplier, and had threatened to take him in. The drug dealer, whose name escaped the memory of all the witnesses, had beaten up his customer, Officer Jack, and had fled. At least that was their story and they were remarkably determined to stick to it.

Jack had been suspended after an internal investigation. His injured back ensured that, when he was finally cleared, he could not return to the profession he had determined to make his life's work from his days in elementary school. But there had been no real effort, on the part of the department, to clear his name. Jack did not have the resources to press his case and wasn't sure he wanted to be reinstated, only to end up driving a desk for the rest of his life, anyway.

He decided he could live for a while, at least, with the black cloud of suspicion hanging over him. But then had come the realization that he still had access to the department. Like Alice, for Jack Elton, circumstances just became curiouser and curiouser.

These thoughts came back to mind as he waited for the officer assigned to accompany him to the home of one of the missing girls.

Jack was delighted when he realized who would accompany him on his trip. It was all he could do to keep from breaking into a broad smile.

He could see that Officer Cummins was enjoying the moment as well. Sometimes, these things are just meant to be.

That had been Jack's sentiment when, six months ago, his friend, Greg, had invited him to a party at his apartment.

"I've got you a date," Greg had said.

Jack had always been irritated by his friends' attempts to set him up with someone. Usually the someone was not compatible and he found that he had to exchange polite dialog through the rest of the evening while others were pairing up or planning more dates.

He had thought, "What on earth has Greg got for me now?" But then his friend had, with a sweeping gesture, indicated the most heavenly creature Jack had seen in a long time.

The stunning young woman had her blond hair in a bun. She was slim and appeared fit. She wore a blue blouse, navy slacks, and a gold badge.

"Jack, meet Officer Valerie Cummins," Greg had said. "You two ought to take some time to get to know each other."

Jack could not have agreed more. Fortunately the feeling had been mutual. He had not seen Val much since then, but had called from time to time. His call the other day—the most recent—had caught her and her partner at a traffic stop.

Jack wanted to know more about this girl, this officer of the law who had so arrested his attention.

Jack was glad of the opportunity to have someone else drive for a change. The past few days, in his cramped little buggy, had taken its toll on his muscles. The roominess of a squad car was a pleasant treat.

He would have to confess, too, to liking the sense of power that traveling in a marked car had always given him.

Folks slowed down when they saw you coming. Sidewalk traffic turned to see where you were headed as you drove by.

Today, he couldn't be sure if it was the car or his chauffeur that made men slow down and look.

Jack always enjoyed the looks from the little kids walking with their parents. They would smile and wave and sometimes call out a greeting to the officers.

Val took her job seriously. Even with her friend she was all business. She wore her blond hair in a bun, just as it had been when Jack first met her. Her make-up was subtle but intended to enhance her beauty. Jack wondered how seriously offenders might take someone who looked as good as she, even in the standard issue police uniform, with the badge and walkie-talkie mike clipped to her epaulet.

He would give her this—she really knew how to maneuver in downtown traffic. As they wove in and out of the cars on the street, he could see that she had learned her lessons well at the police academy.

They spoke very little as Val took them to their ultimate destination. In spite of their blossoming relationship, Jack wasn't sure how she felt about ferrying a civilian around to interrogate people in whom the police had, at least, a passing interest. This was an unusual situation, even for him, but he appreciated the trust his former colleagues still had in him. He really appreciated their choice for accompanying officer and was determined to be professional about it. He resolved to repay the favor by doing the best job of getting all the information he could. And whether this trip solved the case or not, he would not betray their faith in his ability.

It seemed almost certain that the case would not be solved by this visit as he and Officer Cummins rolled up to the front door of the Franklin home. Unless the girl in the morgue had been severely dressing down, or had been disowned years ago, he figured she had never lived here.

Val gave a low whistle as they approached the residence.

A semi-circular driveway led up to the double doors of what could only be called a mansion. A gardener was trimming the hedge and a liveried chauffeur stood beside a very high-class car, with a statue of a winged woman on its radiator.

Well, nothing ventured, nothing gained, Jack thought to himself. "Would you like to join me?" he asked Val, hoping she saw his wink, and heard the smile in his voice.

She gave him a smile, and a look that said, "You can bet your life I want to see inside this place."

She said, "Sure. Let's go."

A gray-haired gentleman in a black suit answered their knock at the door. When he spoke, Jack noticed a clipped British accent. *The quintessential butler,* he thought to himself.

"We'd like to speak to Mr. and Mrs. Franklin. May we come in?"

"Yes, please do. Is this about Rene?"

The two entered a broad foyer. Dark, rich woodwork surrounded them and a marble floor added to the opulent decor. They followed the older man into a sitting room, before Jack responded to the question.

"We'd prefer to speak to the Franklins, if you don't mind." Jack noticed the young police officer giving him a strange look. The reason became apparent with the older gentleman's next words.

"Please sit down. Mrs. Franklin is unavailable at the moment, but you can say whatever it is you must say, to me. I am William Franklin; Rene's father."

"Oh, Mr. Franklin, sir. I didn't know. I mean I assumed. Never mind . . ."

Jack stammered on. Valerie tried hard to stifle a grin.

"Do you have any information about my daughter?" Franklin leaned close to the red-faced investigator. His voice betrayed frustration and anger.

"Well sir," Officer Cummins had obviously decided to take some of the heat off Jack. "We have come to see if you have some details, and perhaps a picture of your daughter, that might help us to give you an answer to that question. How old was Rene?"

"She would have been twenty-three next month."

"Please, sir, we're not ready to assume that she won't be around to celebrate that birthday. What color was her hair? Did she ever dye it?

"She had, I mean has, the most beautiful long dark hair. She has never dyed her hair. Never needed to."

Jack's turn.

"Would she have had any reason to fear for her life, as far as you know?" He knew he was cutting it a little close, and perhaps revealing a few more cards than he ought but the questions needed to be asked.

"Are you suggesting my daughter was mixed up in something unsavory? Tell me, right now. I need to know. Is my daughter dead? It will be the end of her mother if she is."

"Do you have a picture of your daughter," Jack asked.

"I have a family picture over on the mantle. I'm not sure whether it will help at this point. We have a large family and the faces in the photo are a little small."

Mr. Franklin rose from the couch on which he had been sitting, and moved toward the fireplace that took up most of one wall. He reached up to remove a photo in a gold-colored frame. He held it for Jack to see and pointed to the face of a young woman who was standing on the left side of a family gathering.

William Franklin had not lied. The image was so small that it was not easy to make out the features of the girl. It might have been the girl from the office. But Mr. Franklin and the rest of the family were definitely not Asian.

That's not to say she wasn't adopted, Jack reflected.

He looked at the father, trying to estimate how well he might handle the sight of the autopsy photo. It would settle the question once and for all. Jack figured Franklin to be a man of strong constitution.

"I'd like you to look at a picture, sir. It might be your daughter. You may have seen it in the papers."

"We don't read the newspaper much. I probably would not have seen it."

"I must warn you, sir. It's not very good and the subject is, unfortunately, deceased. Do you think you can handle it?"

Jack held out the brown envelope with the photograph.

"Take your time. We're in no rush."

William Franklin took the envelope in both hands. His head dropped and his eyes closed as if he were meditating—or praying about the outcome. Then he turned the envelope over and lifted the flap. With his thumb and forefinger, he grasped the upper edge of the print and eased it slowly out. Jack and his police companion watched the older man's expression.

The photo was almost out of the envelope. Franklin was looking at it intensely. Tears filled his eyes, and a little cry came from his throat. He hung his head, and handed the envelope back to Jack.

Chapter Sixteen

"Sir. Are you okay?" Jack asked.

"Yes. I'll be fine. Give me a minute."

After a moment, the father looked up into the eyes of his two visitors.

"Thank God! That's not my Rene. It's not her. At least I have a little hope she may still be alive. Do you have any idea who that is?" He gestured at the envelope into which Jack was reinserting the photograph of the girl. She would be known as Jane Doe for a little while longer.

"I'm sorry. No, we don't," Jack replied. "I'm happy, for you, that it's not your daughter. I hope you get some resolution to this very soon, Mr. Franklin. We'll be on our way now."

Appropriate courtesies exchanged, Jack and his companion left the mansion and began the drive back to police headquarters.

The meeting over, Jack had the opportunity to concentrate on his driver. Even with the pressure off, she looked to be all business. She handled herself well, from what he could tell of their brief time together with Mr. Franklin. But he noticed, too, that she was all woman and even in uniform she was attractive enough to send hormones streaming through his system, and make him want to see her out of uniform— in a nice dress, perhaps. His mind wandered to thoughts of non-police activities.

"So, if you don't mind, may I ask how long you've been with the force?"

She kept her eyes on the road and the mirrors. "No, I don't mind. I joined the force about seven months ago, right after getting out of the police academy."

"You're not from around here?"

"Nope. Born and raised in Saskatoon. Lived there all my life, until I went off to Regina for my training. Toughest thing I ever did."

"Leaving home, you mean?"

"Police training. There were days I thought I was going to die. There were others when I was afraid I wouldn't, if you know what I mean."

Jack knew well what Officer Cummins meant. He had endured the basic training that challenged you physically, and mentally, for months. Some people didn't make it, and were sent home—a degrading experience for those who thought they were tough enough to be cops. Those who survived the rigorous training left the academy harder physically and mentally, and as well prepared as anyone can be, fresh out of school.

"So you came straight here. How are you liking the big city?"

"It sure is different out here. Things are closer together. I don't think the crime is any different, just a little more centralized."

"You're managing to settle in?"

"Actually, I've had a hard time with that. I don't have a

lot of friends. I got myself a little apartment over on the east side. Stay home most of the time, except when I'm working."

"And when you're out partying, like the night I met you," Jack said.

She looked over at Jack for the first time during the drive and gave him a smile.

"That was my first time out since I came to the city," she said, and smiled at him again. "I had a good time."

Jack's heart skipped a beat. He figured he knew her problem. A girl with Valerie's looks was a threat to the other women officers, and the men would figure they stood no chance with her. They'd also figure she had a boyfriend already. He decided to take a chance.

"I know this great restaurant over by the water. They have great seafood. Would you like to join me sometime? I'm living alone too."

"Gee, that would be nice. I haven't gone anywhere but to fast food places since I moved. Thanks."

She kept her eyes on the road, but smiled again.

"Well, here we are, back at the office. You got a car around here somewhere?" she asked.

"It's probably best if I don't point it out to you just yet. I need to keep up appearances until after our first real date."

"So, there's going to be more than one?" She smiled broadly and looked at Jack, with wide eyes.

"Let's just do this one day at a time, Officer. Where can I get in touch with you, when you're not stopping speeders?"

Jack had only had a cell number until now. He figured that Val had used it as a hedge to keep him from calling her at home if he turned out to be a bore. He hoped that her fears had been alleviated.

Jack got his answer when Officer Cummins tore a sheet

from a notepad attached to the console of the patrol car and scribbled a phone number.

"I'm on day shift for the next little while. Most evenings are good. Actually, any evening away from work and the apartment is good, these days."

"I'll be in touch. My hours are a little crazy, but I'll call you real soon," he said.

Jack walked along the rows of cars in the visitors' lot. His thoughts were distracted from the murder case by the thought of Valerie Cummins, and her winning smile. Finally, he came to his own distinctive set of wheels. He was about to get in when he noticed a slip of paper on the windshield, under one of the wipers.

He freed the small sheet from its restraint and unfolded the note.

"See me when you get back." It was signed, "Willis."

Keegan Willis wants to see me. What have I done to cross him this time, I wonder?

Jack closed and locked the car again, and headed back down the row, to the front door of the police station.

He gained admission to the detective branch and went in search of Willis. The officer was talking on the phone in his office when Jack walked up and looked in the door. The detective motioned for him to come in and sit down, as he continued his conversation.

"Yeah, I think we've got the right one this time. Her father came in and said he recognized her from the picture. I'm quite certain we can solve this if we follow the lead. Look, can I get back to you? I've got someone here with me. I'll let you know what's going on tomorrow."

He hung up and looked quite pleased with himself. "Hi Jack. I see you got my little note."

"What did I do wrong this time, detective?" Jack's brow was deeply furrowed.

"I've got good news."

"Don't tell me. You've saved some big bucks on your auto insurance." Jack smiled.

"Very funny. No. Actually we've had a break in our murder case. That was Brown on the phone. He left earlier for a meeting of some sort. I was here when the girl's old man showed up and ID'd the body."

"You got a positive ID?"

"Yeah, dad looked really broken up when we took him down to the morgue. He said it was his daughter."

"What's her name?"

"I've got it here." He pushed papers around on his desk, looking for the form. It's Japanese actually. She is, let me see. Ah, here it is. Rhonda Fukushima, daughter of Gregory Fukushima and his wife, Noriko."

"What do we know about her?"

"We're still checking things out. I'll have to get back to you with that. I know you think I'm a little overbearing at times but it's just the way I am. I will do what I can to try to help you and your friend, but I have an obligation to do the police work first. Sorry. You're not police anymore."

"I'm touched by your generosity. Seriously. This IS good news," Jack said.

"Your friend still isn't free to leave town, you understand. The girl, here, could still be his victim."

"I think you'll discover that you are wrong to keep thinking he's a suspect. But, I'll let it all go through the channels."

"If anyone is interested, she'll be at Les Sables."

"Come again?"

"The body? Rhonda What's-her-name? She'll be resting,

as they say, at Les Sables Funeral Home over on Fourth. I pity the poor guy that draws that case for embalming. After all this time, without proper pickling, she looks a little messy. Smells worse. The refrigerator down there, in the morgue, can only do so much."

"That's the Willis we all know and love. You have such a sensitive side to you."

"Thanks for noticing. See you tomorrow, will we?"

"You can bet on that."

Jack left the building feeling somewhat buoyed by the news that there was a name for the body. There was still a lot of work to be done and, whether it was him, or the police who sorted it all out, he didn't much care. But he was enjoying the old excitement again. The thrill of the hunt. He could feel the adrenaline. It pursued, and overpowered, the testosterone.

Valerie would have to take a rain check on dinner, but there would be no harm in seeing if she might be willing to drive the Private Investigator guy around a little more, after hours of course, maybe in uniform, to help soften the interviewees' hesitancy to cooperate.

Where had he seen the name? He'd heard or read the name Fukushima somewhere, but couldn't quite pin down where or when. A good bet would be Chinatown, but he wasn't jumping to any conclusions, just yet. And besides, he wasn't all that sure about a Japanese name in a Chinese community.

There would likely be plenty of time to sort that out later. He was feeling hungry again. Why hadn't he invited Valerie to dinner tonight? She had probably left for the day already. The shifts had changed while he was in speaking to Willis. He'd save his money, and eat at home this time. Something French, perhaps. He thought he might have a tin of 'Feves au

Lard' he could cook up. It would go well with a little 'pain grille.'

Beans on toast. Things always sounded much more appealing in French.

Jack pulled out of the parking lot and drove in the direction of the setting sun. His thoughts alternated back and forth between two young women, their faces engraved indelibly on his mind; one cold and dead and lying on a stainless gurney, while preservatives were pumped into her arteries; the other, young and alive, and just as alone as he was tonight. He would deal with them, one at a time.

Jack thought a number of times about calling Valerie that evening. Each time, he managed to convince himself that he didn't want to appear too forward and, perhaps, scare her away. Instead, he ate his beans alone, and sopped up the sauce with slices of toast. His after-dinner beverage was a glass of flat Coke, from a half-used bottle he found in the back of the refrigerator.

Afterward, he went downstairs to his office and unlocked the door. The flashing light on the answering machine reminded him that he had not been in there for some time. Mail had piled up on the floor behind the door, as well.

It was the same old story—bills and the mass-mailed offers to grant him financial favors if he would just fill in the credit card pre-approved application. He wished he had a fireplace for all this junk mail.

Jack pressed the message button on the answering machine. It came as no great surprise that the only messages were from bill collectors who would just have to wait, and collection agencies looking to hire him to deliver paper to those who didn't pay their bills on time. He wondered if there was some way to get the two groups to work together. He jotted down phone numbers and names and resolved to get back to these folks tomorrow, or sometime—soon anyway.

He locked up and went back to his apartment.

He turned on the television and slumped into his favorite chair. There was a police detective show that looked interesting. It had begun seventeen minutes earlier, so he would probably have trouble getting the story line.

Better than nothing, he thought. At least it beat the alternative; thinking what the night could have been like, if he'd only thought a bit faster before getting out of Officer Cummins' patrol car.

As it turned out, it didn't really matter. When Jack awoke, it was well past midnight, and there was someone on TV, selling some new cooking gadget that, they were saying, "Will revolutionize the way you cook potatoes. Order now, and get two for the price of one."

Just what I need; two pieces of junk to clutter my already cluttered kitchen.

Jack reflected on how he, almost single-handedly, had helped to sustain the television product marketing industry. He had a house full of products, all gathering dust, to prove it.

He stood up unsteadily and turned off the TV.

He was asleep almost as soon as his head hit the pillow. He dreamed about a young female patrol officer with a great smile, and her hair in a bun.

Chapter Seventeen

Early the next morning, Jack drove to the police station. He found the chief detective in his office, a pile of folders spread over his desk.

Ted Brown outlined the few details the investigators had been able to glean from Gregory, the girl's father.

"It's been a little bit hard getting all the facts straight. Dad doesn't have as good a grasp on the English language as we might have liked. Here's what we've pieced together so far."

Jack learned that Rhonda was twenty-seven years old. She had held a number of low-paying jobs since arriving in the city with her parents, from Fukuoka, Japan, approximately ten years earlier.

Rhonda had worked the fast-food chains, for a while, to raise money for a college education. It was uncertain whether she had actually finished the course. At one point she had been a store clerk, but had quit for reasons unknown. Her resume included a number of part-time secretarial positions.

"The family is still very Old World, if you know what I mean. Dad is the head of the family. He has all the authority. Mom helps out with the family business," Brown said.

"They kept a close rein on the daughter?" Jack asked.

"She was the only child. I gather they tried very hard to insulate her from western culture, but dad was a little distressed. She was apparently not as pliable as he would have liked. She started hanging around with young people she met at work."

"Strong willed, eh?"

"So it would seem," the detective replied.

"Any reason why she might have ended up in Biggs' office?"

Brown's forehead wrinkled. "I think dad is holding back on me. I'm not sure if he knows anything or not. Might have to go at things from another angle."

"Got a plan?" Jack asked. His head went to one side like an old dog responding to his master's voice. The eyebrows raised.

"We've got some leads on the folks she used to hang out with. I thought we might track some of them down and just have a little chat over coffee."

"Is it okay if I have a chat with her father? I'd like to get some information from him about what might have happened. I've got a couple of folks who've said they're willing to come along with me. They're from the department. That will keep you in the loop, so to speak."

Jack was thinking about Valerie Cummins again, but realized that Ron Leung might be the more efficient choice, under the circumstances.

"Sure, you can talk to him. But if you come up with anything, I want to know about it. Deal?" Brown asked.

"Sure. Not a problem. Just one more thing. Where can I

find Mr. Fukushima? Where does he work? You mentioned that it was a family business."

"See, Jack, that's why we need a police force. So regular citizens can go out and solve crimes. We get the details; you go searching for the clues."

"Okay, Mr. Answer Man, what does dad do for a living?"

"You've probably seen his shop, Jack. He owns a little import/export place, on the main drag, in the center of town. Place called—now, get this for originality—Fukushima's."

A light went on somewhere in Jack's brain. He knew, now, why the name was familiar. He had seen the little shop before. It had been a point of interest recently. An image shot into his brain and, just as quickly, fled away again.

"Thanks, Ted. I owe you one. I may have Ron Leung with me, if you're looking for him. I hope he's around. I may need his translating skills."

"Can't help you, Jack." Detective Leung had a look of genuine regret on his face.

"You're tied up?"

"Look at me, Jack. I'm Chinese. He's Japanese. We don't speak the same language."

Jack looked closely at his friend. He had to admit that he knew very little about the difference in physical appearance between the two nationalities. He wondered whether that acknowledgment didn't brand him somehow.

"I know a little about geography. The guy's from Fukuoka. It's close to China. Maybe he's picked up a little Chinese along the way," Jack said.

"Do you realize how many dialects there are in China? You might as well take along someone born right here. You'll have that much success communicating."

Jack thought about the other officer that had offered to be

with him when he spoke to Gregory Fukushima. She probably wouldn't be able to help much with translating, but he was sure she would make him feel better about his inability to get the Japanese gentleman to articulate what he knew.

He soon thought better of his idea. He would have a hard time rationalizing the move if anyone decided to question the wisdom of a civilian taking a uniformed officer away from her assigned duties. Besides, her presence might skew his reasoning ability, and break his concentration, as he tried to communicate with Rhonda's father.

Jack drove to the main street, where the row of souvenir and specialty shops that served the tourist population stretched along one side. He reflected on the last time he had passed this way. It seemed so long ago, yet it had been less than two weeks. He recollected that morning when the fog was in his brain, rather than hovering over the harbor. Memories of the seeds of that day's hangover returned, as he looked at the stores in broad daylight.

It was easy to find Fukushima's. A large neon sign proclaimed the store's existence and a sandwich board on the sidewalk directed potential customers with a large red arrow.

Pedestrian traffic moved back and forth across the front of the store but, today at least, it did not appear that too many were attracted by either the signs or the gaudy display of wares in the window.

There were the T-shirts, proclaiming that the wearer had visited the city, or had been given the piece of apparel by someone who had. There were some hideously colored animé sport shirts that attracted the teenage crowd, both tourists and locals. As well, one could purchase bamboo tables and wicker ware. Statues of Buddha in various postures, sizes, and colors were also displayed. Inside the store, Jack noticed that the walls were covered with a variety of imported items. Pegboards held hooks that, in turn, supported various trinkets in plastic bags. Some proclaimed Souvenir of Canada in bold letters, while little gold-colored seals declared Made in Japan, or some other East Asian country.

Gregory Fukushima was a short man with his black hair slicked back in an attempt to cover the development of a balding spot. He was assisting a young woman with her purchase of a string of beads.

As Jack listened, it was apparent that the communication problem might not be as severe as he had been led to believe. Indeed, the businessman had a strong accent and sometimes pronounced words in an unusual way or with the wrong emphasis. But, except for the occasional stumble, Jack found it relatively easy to eavesdrop on the brief transaction that was taking place before him. He decided to look around the store until Mr. Fukushima had a free moment.

It was not lost on Jack that the proprietor's dark eyes followed him as he moved away, and down one of the aisles lined with shirts, and other paraphernalia. Obviously, this man had been a victim of those taking the 'five-fingered discount' before. Signs were posted all over the city, reminding people that it was a criminal offense to shoplift, and that prosecution would be swift and severe for anyone caught with stolen merchandise. Every year, though, the local business association reported that shoplifting was cutting into their profits and forcing prices higher. Jack stuffed his hands in his pockets to reassure the store owner that he meant no ill.

A short while later, Jack was aware of a presence at his elbow.

"May I be . . . assistance to you?"

"Yes, I believe you can." Jack smiled at Gregory Fukushima. "My name is Jack Elton, and I am so sorry to hear about your daughter."

The old man's eyes were cast down, and he said, simply, "Yes, my Ronnie, she is gone."

"Would it be possible for me to ask you a few questions? I'm trying to help find the one responsible for your daughter's death."

The man shook his head slowly. Jack wasn't sure whether it was an expression of sadness, or an indication that he couldn't, or wouldn't, help.

"Come," the shopkeeper said, as he moved to a space at the back of the store, where Jack could see a small table with a couple of rickety chairs. A small electric kettle sat on one corner, and a china teapot and two small cups had been placed in the center.

A simple hand gesture indicated that Jack should sit. Fukushima took the remaining chair. He looked satisfied that his hospitality was appreciated. The man gave a nod to his visitor.

"Now, sir, I'd like to know a little more about your daughter. It might help us solve this case and bring it to a close," Jack said.

"All I want is honor for my family," the man replied.

"Yes, I can understand that, sir. We intend to do the best we can."

"My Ronnie, Rhonda, was nice girl. Sometimes disobedient. Sometimes respectful. Sometimes turning from what her mother and I teach her."

"I'm sure all children are like that sometimes. Can you tell me about her friends?" Jack asked.

"Many friends. Boys. Some good. Some not so good. One very bad, I think. Girls good mostly. People she work with. Some she know from school."

"You say one of her boy friends was very bad. Was he in trouble with the law?"

"Don't know. Was disrespectful of elders and dishonored my daughter, I think. She learned disrespect from him."

"Do you think he might be responsible for your daughter's death?"

"Know. It."

"What was his name? Do you mind telling me?" Jack asked.

"A Mr. Heddon. Jimmie, she called him. He was not nice to me. Yelled a lot. My Ronnie never disrespected elders until that Heddon man came along."

People were coming into the store and milling about. Fukushima was obviously a little anxious to keep an eye on things. Jack couldn't force him to stay, but he knew the old man was too respectful to get up in the middle of the conversation.

"Tell you what, sir. I can see that you are going to be busy for awhile. I'll be going now. Would it be all right if I came back another time?"

The old man nodded. "Yes. All right. You come back. We talk. You have tea." He motioned to the makeshift tea service on the little table.

After a few more exchanges, Jack stood. The other man rose and gave a little bow before turning to his customers.

As he left, Jack saw the proprietor showing a selection of T-shirts to a couple and their young son. As the man spoke, his eyes scanned the other customers, ever vigilant.

Jack planned to track down this Heddon guy and see what his story was. The old man had seemed quite certain that the boy had played some part in the murder of the girl. He had given Jack a slip of paper, with a phone number and an address on it, before the two had parted company.

Jimmie was working, the worried female voice at the end

of the line reported, and would not be home until later in the day.

Another night out and about, Jack thought. *No date tonight, I guess.*

Jack hung up the pay phone, and put the note in his pocket. Then he patted himself down to find his car keys. He drove up the street to the office tower that housed Biggs, Wilberforce, Hutton, and Small. He needed to talk to his friend and, maybe, some of Brendan's staff.

Chapter Eighteen

It was approaching the noon hour, and the lobby was full of people, coming and going. The bank on the main floor was doing a brisk business. *I wonder how much they will make in service charges, this morning,* Jack mused as he walked toward the row of elevators in the center of the lobby.

He joined the crowd waiting for the next one to arrive. Like others before him, he pressed the 'up' button a number of times before he was confident that the message had been sent. Once the doors opened, everyone piled in as if this was the last elevator of the day. They stood shoulder-to-shoulder and, one by one, called their floor numbers to the person closest to the control panel, a short gray-haired woman who looked too frail to be traveling like this. *The altitude might kill her,* Jack thought, with a smile.

By the time he arrived at the eleventh floor, most of his companions had got off. The little old lady had traveled one floor and had been replaced by a long-legged girl in a short dress.

The offices of Biggs, Wilberforce, Hutton, and Small were busy, and popular, by the looks of things. The hustle and bustle of deadlines kept folks moving in and out of cubicles. Groups huddled over artwork that needed to be finalized. Phone conversations were conducted in hushed tones until a client's joke needed to be laughed at, in order to indicate that someone was paying attention.

Abba deBie looked as if the shock of her discovery, on that fateful day, not more than a week ago, had faded. She was still filing, phoning, planning, and conferring with her colleagues.

From the reception area, it was impossible to tell whether Brendan was in his office. Jack turned to the young woman behind the counter and introduced himself.

"Jack Elton. Is Mr. Biggs around?"

"Oh I know who you are, Mr. Elton. I saw you about a week ago when . . ." Her eyes glazed over only briefly. "Just a moment, I'll let Mr. Biggs know you are here."

She disappeared around the corner of the wall that separated the reception area from the rest of the office.

"Jack. Good to see you. Come on into my office."

Brendan Biggs was looking as if he had got some rest since Jack had last seen him, after picking him up at the jail. They walked between the rows of cubicles until they came to Biggs' lair overlooking the harbor.

"What's new Jack?" Brendan was sounding very upbeat.

"We've got a name for the girl. We might have a solid lead about a suspect. And you're still under suspicion," Jack replied.

"How can that be, if there's another suspect?"

"All I know is you still can't leave town in a hurry, or someone will be hot on your tail. I think you know who I mean. I don't expect it will be much longer, but keep an eye on what you do, and don't act suspiciously."

"Right you are, Mr. Bond. Is there anything else I can do to take the focus off myself?"

"Are you . . . have you continued to be faithful to Meagan?"

"They think I was having some sort of liaison with this woman who showed up dead?" Brendan looked aghast.

"Specifically, she showed up dead right outside this office. She had stab wounds all over her chest. That means she knew her attacker. The coroner found a note in her pocket with your name and this floor number. It looks like she had an appointment with you. Your security guard remembers her saying she was coming up to meet with you. How do you explain that?"

"I can't. I didn't recognize her. What did you say her name was?"

Brendan could sound very convincing, Jack thought. But then, that was what he was paid to do. His job was to convince people that this product, or that, was the best there is. If he didn't, he'd soon be out of work. He could be lying through his teeth but, on the other hand, Jack was not convinced that his friend ever lied to sell a product. His reputation for winning with the facts was legendary.

Jack would track down the Heddon boy tonight.

"Can I interest you in lunch?" Jack asked. "You're paying."

"I guess I do owe you some compensation, Jack, don't I?"

"This won't bring us anywhere near even, Brendan, but it will be a start. I think I'm going to have to spend a few more days on this case before I'm done."

Brendan cleared folders from his desk and passed them to a clerk, to be re-filed, as he and Jack walked back to the front of the office.

"I don't suppose McDonald's is going to be good enough today?"

Jack laughed as he pushed open one of the heavy glass doors that led into the hallway. He pressed the elevator button and bowed ceremoniously when the door opened. With a sweeping motion of his hand, he ushered his friend into the coach for the quick trip to street level.

Jack chose a booth in the wood-paneled interior of the high-class restaurant Brendan had taken him to. The seats were covered in leather burnished to a high shine by the backsides of the many customers who had visited during the eatery's long existence. A candle burned in a glass holder in the center of the table. The silverware was really silver, and the tablecloth and napkins were linen. A log was burning in the fireplace.

A young man approached them. In one hand he held two stemmed water goblets. In the other was a silver water jug. Under his arm were two menus. He deftly filled the glasses and placed one in front of each of the men.

With his now free hand, he whipped the menus from under his arm and with a flourish, presented them to Jack and Brendan.

"Your server, Marissa, will be with you shortly. Can I get you something to drink before your meal?" He was poised to take their order.

"I'll just have coffee for now," said Jack.

"Me too."

When the young man had gone, Brendan leaned forward and asked, conspiratorially, "What now?"

"Well, now we wait for Marissa; she of the order pad and pen. Then I order an obscenely expensive lunch, which you will pay for. After that, we will return to whatever activity excites or compels us."

"You know what I mean. What happens with the case of my dead, late-night visitor?"

At that moment, Marissa showed up table-side with a bright smile and an order pad.

"Have you gentlemen decided what you would like, or do you need a few more minutes?"

From the unopened menus before them, it was evident that they might need a little more time. The conversation was suspended as they perused a lengthy list of appetizers and entrees.

The choices were finally made. Marissa, who had been hovering in the background, appeared beside them and recorded their orders for the kitchen staff.

Jack picked up the thread of the earlier conversation.

"You are relatively young. I would venture to say you are well off. Guys like you don't tend to have a problem with women. It's not unheard-of for executives like yourself to take advantage of that sort of notoriety. The cops are bound to wonder whether this girl was a friend of yours."

"I swear to you, I've never met the girl. I have never, ever, had contact with her." Brendan's eyes were wide. His complexion was reddening.

"I don't suppose you'd heard that she was pregnant. Someone might have wanted her dead because of that. The police are going to wonder whether you had erred—might have wanted a mistake out of the way."

"Like I said, I don't know her. Never met her." Brendan's voice had risen an octave or two as he spoke. "You haven't even told me her name."

"Fukushima."

"I beg your pardon?"

"That's her name. Rhonda Fukushima. I spoke to her father. He owns the shop down on main street, Fukushima's."

"Sounds logical to me." Brendan smiled.

"Dad says there is a guy she was going with who might be responsible. I've got to check him out. He may be the one who gets you off the hook for good."

"I have to confess that the past few days have been real hard. I've tried to keep my mind on my work, so that I wouldn't have to think too much."

"Can you think of anyone who might have it in for you?" Jack asked.

Brendan looked toward the ceiling and rubbed the right side of his face. A look of concentration came over him.

"I can think of lots of people who would like to take some of my clients away from the company. I don't think any of them would stage a murder in my office, though."

"There isn't a jealous boyfriend out there, somewhere, who's ticked that you've been romancing his sweetie?"

"I told you before. I'm not like that—anymore."

"Which one is having the steak?" Marissa was back with the food. Jack cleared a place in front of himself.

"Good," she said. "Then the seafood platter must be yours. Enjoy your meals, gentlemen. Can I heat up your coffee for you?"

They said yes, and Marissa did. She retreated into the background.

The conversation was very limited for the next few minutes as the two friends wolfed down their meal. They commented occasionally about the quality of the food. Marissa came around to see if everything was okay, and refilled their cups several times.

Finally, the meal was over and they sat back feeling, and looking, satisfied. Both turned down the dessert menu. The two men engaged in some small talk while they waited for the bill.

"I must say, you're a really good cook," Jack commented to the young waitress.

When it finally dawned on her that he was trying to make a joke, Marissa's face went pink, and she went away, giggling, with Brendan's credit card.

"I'm at a loss as to why the girl ended up in your office. It's a question that haunts me," Jack said.

"I'm not comfortable with it either, you know," Brendan said.

"I mean, who gave her directions to your office, and why did she so willingly go at night? Was she expecting to meet someone from your company?"

"Dunno." Brendan drained his coffee cup, and reached for his pen to sign the credit card slip that the waitress had brought to the table. He scribbled his signature and began to slide out of the booth.

"I wonder if the boyfriend will be of any help," Jack asked.

He slid out and joined his friend, who was heading for the door.

"Let me know what you find out," Brendan said as they headed back to the office tower. "I'm anxious to put this all behind me and move on."

"I'm sure the Fukushima family is wishing they could get past this too. It is sure to be tougher on them for some time to come."

"I don't want to appear insensitive to their plight. Their situation is understandably different from mine. I wouldn't want to compare the two situations." Brendan sounded genuinely remorseful.

"Now, of course, I'm trying to solve this thing for you *and* them. A little added pressure won't do me any harm, I suppose."

"I appreciate your help, Jack. Really I do."

The two men parted company outside the office tower.

Valerie Cummins' shift would be coming to an end soon. Maybe she and Jack could run into each other by accident, and he could renew his invitation to dinner by the water.

Jack hoped she could lend some of her own expertise to solving the case, as well. It wouldn't hurt to ask.

Chapter Nineteen

Jack felt like a schoolboy hanging around outside a girl's house, hoping she will come outside and notice him. The air was cool but the afternoon sun beating down on the little car was gradually raising the temperature of the interior. Jack rolled down the window.

Patrol cars arrived and parked in the police lot. Every now and then a couple of officers in uniform would leave the building and drive away for their shift. Jack watched the exchanges take place. A couple of vehicles in. A patrol car out.

The K-9 unit van arrived, and the officer went to the rear to let out his dog. He set down a bowl, and emptied his water bottle into it. The animal, with tail wagging enthusiastically, lapped up the liquid and sat, as if waiting for more. The handler patted his companion, scratched behind the dog's ear, clipped a lead to its collar, and the two began walking toward the building.

The German shepherd wore a special bulletproof vest with the police logo on each shoulder. Jack wondered what sort of person would want to shoot a police dog, and then he remembered some of the folks he had had to deal with when he was on the force. It seemed he had answered his own question.

"I'm sorry sir, you're not allowed to sleep in the visitor parking lot at this time of day."

The familiar voice brought a broad smile to Jack's face.

"Why Officer Cummins, you must be working under cover. You crept up on me, and I didn't even see you."

"No, not really. While you were watching the puppy over there, I was coming out the door. You've gotta remember to keep your focus."

"You think I was waiting for you?"

"I'd kinda hoped so. What were you really doing?" Valerie asked.

"Truth?"

"I'm the law, buster."

"I was waiting for you. I just wanted to see you. I just wanted to know that yesterday wasn't just wishful thinking on my part."

"Nope. I still get hungry. I still hate sitting at home waiting to go to bed. You're still the first guy who invited me to dinner. Is tonight the night?" she asked.

"I wish it could be, but I've got some more business to do with that murder. I suppose you heard that we at least know who the girl is. I've got a lead I need to follow up. I don't suppose you're up for some fast food and a little more police work."

"If I don't have to sit at home alone for a few hours or make out report forms, I'll follow you anywhere. Check that *almost* anywhere. I can use the companionship," Val said.

She indicated the building across from the parking lot.

"In there," she continued, "I'm just another officer and, when work is done, all the relationships end until my next shift. I feel like I haven't got a friend in this town. But then, here you are."

"It's too early for dinner, and the guy I need to see probably won't be out of work for a while yet. What shall we do?"

"Is it casual or formal, this fast food place you're thinking about?" she asked.

"Definitely casual."

"You still got my number? Call me when you're ready, and I'll give you directions to my place. You do have a cell phone, don't you?"

Val gave Jack the directions and he wrote them on the back of the note with her number. He promised to find a pay phone, and call her, before he showed up. She gave him a sorry look over the fact that he was not keeping up with the times, telephonically speaking.

Jack resolved to check into cell phones as soon as he could afford the expense. It might have a positive effect on his love life, as well as his business. That was becoming clearer with each passing day.

"Hi there. I'm on my way over to your place. You got any idea what wine goes with a double cheeseburger?"

"I'll be waiting for you. I've got a pretty good idea what your car looks like. Drive carefully. I can't bail you out if you get pulled over for driving a mechanically unsafe vehicle."

Jack hung up the phone and checked the change slot. It was a habit he had developed as a youngster.

One day he had been out with his parents, shopping. He had looked in the coin return and found a quarter. Ever since, he had never been able to resist digging around in one of those things to see if someone had forgotten something.

* * *

Valerie Cummins lived in an apartment building that looked like a lot of others. Its outward appearance was unremarkable. Unadorned, stuccoed exterior. No balconies. Small windows. No lawn to speak of. Uninteresting views from every apartment. The only saving grace was that this was a part of the city where the trees had not yet been removed, in the name of progress, from along the roadway. The street was shaded by a number of impressive looking oaks.

Val was waiting on the front walkway when he pulled up. She had chosen faded jeans and a pink blouse with the shirt tails tied in a knot at the waist. Her hair was in a pony tail. Jack could see that she had not yet succumbed to the trend of piercing belly buttons.

Casual but appealing, Jack thought, as he watched her walk toward the car. He reached over to open the door for her. Getting out and holding the door was for more formal occasions, he figured.

"Hi. Where are we going?" she asked, smiling, and bouncing slightly on the passenger seat.

"There's a little Mexican place I like, over on the east side. They serve good food and it's cheap—excuse me—inexpensive. We can go from there to my interview."

"Okay, let's go." Another bounce. Another smile. She was enjoying the change in her schedule.

"Not so fast, young lady." Jack tried to sound stern. "I notice you're not wearing your seat belt. Don't you know that seat belts prevent injuries in the event of an accident? You could get us both in deep trouble if we were ever stopped by the police."

"Oh, I am sorry sir. I never realized. Thank you for warning me. I'll never forget my seat belt, ever again."

"You sound well practiced," Jack said, with a smile.

"I hear it a lot around here. Of course, they don't call me 'sir,' but the rest of it is pretty much verbatim."

"Let's not talk shop for awhile. I'll try to make this seem as much like a real date as I can."

"Oh. You mean that this isn't strictly business? If I'd known, I might never have agreed to come with you." Val smiled.

"You are teasing, right?" Jack smiled back.

"Silly!" She threw her head back and laughed.

Watching her enjoy herself gave Jack a sensation he had not experienced often. If this was love, he did not want to do anything to stifle the emotion.

"I really want to make a good impression, you know," Jack said, trying not to sound too serious.

Valerie said nothing, but smiled and twisted the knot at her waist.

They continued across town and finally pulled up at a parking meter across from the little Mexican restaurant that inhabited a low-lying building. From the outside, it was unimpressive. Walking through the door was like crossing the border from southern California. The decor, the music, and the attire of the servers, gave the little place a ring of authenticity.

They were seated at a heavy wooden table with a bright tablecloth. High-backed ladder chairs were solid and allowed them the flexibility to change their seating arrangement. Jack thought it best to stay across the table from his guest for tonight at least.

There would be other, more intimate occasions, he hoped, when they would sit closer without the distraction of other patrons, or the thought of an impending interrogation.

The service was a bit slow. Jack pretended to be the authority on Mexican culture, and suggested that the idea of mañana was the cause for the delay.

"It's just a very easygoing way of life. We might have to wait for days," he smiled.

"I know we said we weren't going to talk business right away, but I need some preparation here, if I'm going to be of any help," Val said. "And you know, of course, I have no more authority, off duty and out of uniform, than you do."

Maybe not, Jack thought, but the officer was definitely on the case, by the sound of it.

"I'm well aware of that," he said. "And I'm sure you're a good cop, but I just wanted the opportunity to be with you. Any insight you might have, or question you might ask this boy, would just be icing on the cake, if you know what I mean."

"So tell me what I'm walking into here," Val continued.

"This guy—James Heddon's his name—is, or rather was, a friend of Rhonda Fukushima, the dead girl.

"Dad seems to feel that Jimmie is responsible for his daughter's death. The boy is disrespectful of his elders, something the Japanese culture that Mr. Fukushima still honors tends to frown on. He thinks the guy wasn't nice to his daughter either. She was pregnant, according to Doc Walle."

"And you figure this Jimmie is just going to up and confess that he's the one, and that will be it?" Val asked.

"I'm not that naive. I'm not even sure yet that he is the one who is responsible. Say, you are starting to sound very businesslike. Better cut that out. Guys won't think you're any fun."

"Sorry. Don't you think I'm any fun?" She pouted.

"I haven't quite gotten around to checking that out yet. Give me time. We may have to keep company for awhile so I can form a definite opinion."

"I think I might like that." The pout was gone.

* * *

Their waiter eventually arrived and went through all the necessary activities leading up to a successful order. Now that the process was begun, things seemed to move a little more quickly.

In the interim, they were plied with an endless supply of tortilla chips and salsa. They both chose to use the hot sauce and drank large amounts of water. By the time their choices arrived, they were already feeling quite full. When they were through, they headed back to the car for the drive to the home of James Heddon.

"That was very nice. Thank you, Jack."

"The night's not over yet. Don't thank me until we've had our little tête-à-tête with the boyfriend."

They drove on in silence.

Chapter Twenty

The address that Jack had been given for Jimmie Heddon led him and Valerie to a part of town that featured some of the older character homes. Heddon's house had a veranda that spanned the front of the building. It had clapboard siding, painted white with green trim. The small front lawn was home to an oak tree that offered shade from the summer sun and likely sheltered the walkway from the storms of winter.

They moved slowly up the cracked concrete walkway and climbed to the front porch on creaking wooden stairs. Jack knocked on the door and was surprised to be greeted by an older woman with graying hair. She wore a print dress and an apron, on which she wiped her hands before opening the screen door.

"May I help you?" she asked, looking from one to the other.

"My name is Jack Elton, and this is Valerie Cummins. We're doing a little bit of investigation into the death of a young woman. We're looking for a James Heddon. Does he live here?"

"My boy doesn't know anything about that sort of thing.

159

What is the meaning of your coming around here and stirring up trouble."

She started to close the door.

"I take it you are James' mother, then?"

The door stopped.

"Yes, that's right. This is awful. I don't know what to think. My Jimmie just wouldn't be involved in something like that. I think you should go, now."

"Mama, who's at the door? What's wrong?" A man in his twenties came up behind the woman and looked at the visitors. He stood about five-foot-nine, and appeared to be of average weight. He had the appearance of someone who either worked out or had a job with a lot of heavy lifting. His hair was close-cropped. He wore a T-shirt and denims. Jack figured he could still take him on, if it came to that.

"Are you James?" Jack asked, trying to sound as friendly as possible, for the sake of the older woman.

"What's this all about, Jim. I told them you didn't know anything about this," the mother interjected.

"Don't know about what?" The young man moved around his mother and stared at the visitors, hands on hips.

"About the death of Rhonda Fukushima," Jack replied. "She was found in a downtown office, a week or so ago, and we're hoping to get some information from people who knew her."

Jack was trying very hard not to appear to be making any accusations.

The young man's look of distress did not wane.

"It's okay, Mom. Let them come in. I know who they're talking about. Remember? I used to talk about my friend from the temp agency? Open the door, Mom."

The woman looked dubious about opening her house to these two strangers, but backed away to let her son direct them into the living room.

Jack didn't know what to make of this show of co-operation and respect. Either Gregory Fukushima had been thinking of somebody else, or this young man was putting on a great show for the investigators. Time would tell.

"Would anyone like some tea? I have the kettle on."

"No, ma'am, we just had something. But thanks." Valerie was still recuperating from all the water she had drunk to quell the salsa fires of not more than an hour ago. Jack gave her a sly wink.

The older woman retreated to the kitchen, leaving her son to fend for himself.

Jack turned to the young man. "May I call you James?"

"Jimmie's good."

"Jimmie, you knew Rhonda Fukushima well, did you?"

"Yeah, pretty well. Who wants to know?"

That's the boy, Jimmie. Show your true colors, Jack thought.

"I'm sorry. We never introduced ourselves. You must think we're terribly impolite. I'm Jack. This is Valerie. We're doing some investigation work on behalf of a friend of mine. We don't represent the police—not tonight at least."

James looked at his visitors quizzically, but said nothing.

Jack continued, "I've spoken to Rhonda's father, and he told me you and Rhonda were something of an item."

"What of it?" Jimmie cared for mom but didn't give much respect to anyone else, it appeared.

Jack kept his voice level. "Well, Jimmie, you probably know that Rhonda's dead. We need to know whether you have any knowledge of who might have done it. Maybe you can help us with this. Do you know of any reason why Rhonda might have been in the offices of Biggs, Wilber-force, and Hutton and Small, on the night she died, with a note in her pocket saying she was to meet Mr. Biggs?"

"I don't know. Maybe she was looking for work. She was always going to these weird interviews for jobs, trying to get better pay—stuff like that. Some of her girlfriends might be able to help you better than I can. She didn't tell me much about it 'cause I thought some of the places she went weren't the sort of job she should be involved in."

"Can you give us some names? Phone numbers? Anything like that?" Jack asked.

"I'll do what I can. Give me a sec, I'll go get my address book."

When he had gone, Valerie looked at Jack. "Not quite what I had expected. Have you changed your mind about him?"

"Not completely, yet. He's able to convince his mother that he is the son she believes him to be. But he's out romancing the girls and getting himself and them in trouble. He's polite and respectful of mom, but apparently rages out of control at an old man who has different beliefs. I'm waiting to see what happens when we get down to his alibi."

A sound like thundering hooves, coming down the stairs from the second floor, heralded the arrival of Jimmie, with what turned out to be a real 'little black book.'

"Got some paper? I can give you some names and numbers," he said.

Valerie pulled out a note pad from her back pocket and produced a pen from the fanny pack that she carried like a purse. Jimmie dictated the names of a half dozen girls who hung around with Rhonda.

"One of them will probably have some idea why she was there at that time of night," he said.

"Now, I've got to ask one last question, Jimmie," Jack said, after Val had completed her note. "Where were you on the night Rhonda died?"

The change in the boy's countenance was immediate. His face flushed, and he moved threateningly in Jack's direction.

"You're accusing me of killing my girl? Is that what you're doing? I had nothing to do with it. I wasn't even with her that night." The boy's anger was rising with each passing moment.

"You seem to have a bit of a chip on your shoulder, Jimmie."

"I'm feeling a little ticked. No, more than ticked that you'd come in here and accuse me of a thing like that. I think it's time for you two to go. Unless you have some sort of a warrant, I have nothing else to say."

The young man ushered them out of the living room and held the door wide. Jack and Valerie left the house. He watched after them as they walked to the sidewalk.

Just before they pulled away, Jack heard him call back over his shoulder, "Yes, Mom. They're just leaving now. Everything's fine now. I'll be right in."

Jack put the car in gear, and headed back to Valerie's apartment building. Jimmie Heddon had just moved to the head of the line of suspects. Of course, right now, it was a very short line.

"I'd say Jimmie is your prime suspect, Jack." Valerie was looking straight ahead.

"I'm starting to think you're right. Mr. Fukushima seemed positive, when I talked to him too. We have a bit of a communication problem but not as bad as I'd suspected. He seemed certain that Jimmie was the cause of Rhonda's death. I think I should pay another visit to his shop and ask a few more questions."

"You do that, Jack. Although, I suspect some of my colleagues have asked all the questions they need.

"Personally, I've never met the guy," Valerie added. "But,

keep all your options open. Young Mr. Heddon gave you some leads that you should follow, even if you do think that you have your perpetrator. There's always the chance that someone was jealous that Rhonda and Jimmie were going out together. Maybe one of these girls wanted to have him all to herself, and then the pregnancy pushed her over the edge. It meant that the man she wanted might be forced into a permanent relationship with Rhonda. I don't know. I'm just thinking out loud."

"I can see I've got a few more late nights before this thing is finally over." Jack rubbed his eyes with the back of his hand. "What happened back there, tonight, didn't make it any easier for Brendan Biggs, either. Until we can prove otherwise, or someone just up and confesses, I guess he's on the hook a little longer."

"Well, look on the bright side. It gives us the opportunity to see each other a little more as we do our fieldwork. Tonight wasn't a total loss."

Jack smiled. Though the shadows were lengthening, there was still some light to cheer him.

By the time they pulled up in front of Valerie's building, the sun had set, and the streetlights had come on. Jack couldn't just let her out and drive away.

He opened his door, went around to the passenger side, and offered Valerie his hand. She took it, without hesitation, and he helped her to the sidewalk. They walked up the walkway to the front door, arm-in-arm.

"Thanks for coming with me tonight. I appreciated your company," Jack said.

"Thanks for dinner. It was good to be any place other than sitting at home all night. I didn't mean that the way it sounded. I mean I'm glad I spent the evening with you. I'll keep an eye on the parking lot when I come out from work, from now on. And I'm looking forward to a dinner, without the interrogation afterward, sometime soon."

"I'll be watching for you too."

Jack gave her a gentle hug, and Valerie went inside.

As he returned to his car, he was wondering what the future might hold, not only for his case, but also for his relationship with the woman behind the badge.

The empty apartment proved to be almost more than Jack could bear. It seemed colder and emptier than it had ever felt, after the warmth of companionship earlier in the evening. He had to admit that Valerie was making a definite impression. He hoped he might be able to maintain proper perspective, so as not to compromise the work that still had to be done. She was becoming a friend. Perhaps she would become more than that. For now, she was a valuable ally in his quest for the answers to a problem that just seemed to become more complicated with time.

Chapter Twenty-one

J ack headed out to continue his quest, the next morning. The address Jimmie Heddon had given him turned out to be an office building in the center of town. It contained a number of small businesses, one of which was a temporary placement agency.

The Northern Inter-City Placements office was on the first floor of the building. From what Jack could see, it consisted of a small reception area, with three small rooms labeled 'Interviews.' A woman Jack estimated to be about forty, sat at the reception desk, focused on a computer screen. Her eyes alternated between that and a clipboard with, what he assumed, was a fresh application for employment.

The woman's fingers moved over the keys with ease as she entered the data. She was obviously a permanent fixture here.

A nervous looking young girl sat in one of the seats across from the reception area. She was dressed for success, or at least for an interview. She alternated between nibbling on a fingernail and smoothing the skirt of her dress. She fidgeted, as if unused to this style of clothing. Likely, the form belonged to her, Jack figured.

The woman at the keyboard did not look up. It was obvious to Jack that, if he wanted some assistance, he would have to wait.

"Hi there," he said to the girl. Her eyes flickered in his direction, then fled away. "You looking for work?" he asked.

An energetic nod, but nothing verbal. This girl was going to need to develop her conversational skills if she was looking to be a receptionist, or any other job that might require interaction with the public. He decided not to pursue the monologue further.

The keyboard clicked away. The typist flipped over to the next page and continued. The young girl bit her lower lip and crossed and uncrossed her ankles as she stared at the floor.

The data entry seemed to go on forever. By the looks of it, these youngsters were giving the story of their lives for the privilege of a few hours of gainful employment.

Eventually, the young woman's agony came to an end. She was called to the counter, and told that she would be contacted if there was work. It was too late in the morning for anything to materialize today, but she should be ready to go early in the morning, in case she was called. The other option was to show up at the office early and sit, hoping something suitable would come along. Folks called in sick. Women went into labor. Some employees just decided to take a day off and would make some excuse. It was these folk, or rather their employers, who kept the temp business financially viable.

After the girl left, the woman at the computer finally directed her attention to Jack. To her inquiry of how she might help him, he offered the girl's name Jimmie had given him.

"She's out working today. You can find her at, let's see now . . ." She gave Jack a name and address, and added, "Please try not to disturb her while she's working. Since it's only a temporary job, she can be let go for not appearing to pull her weight. Try to arrange to see her during a planned break."

Jack thanked the woman, and gave her every assurance that he would be careful.

As he left the building, another hopeful soul turned up, in a car more dilapidated than Jack's. The young kid who stepped out into the parking lot wore work boots and well-faded jeans. Above the belt, he was adorned with a blue flannel shirt with the sleeves rolled up. A baseball cap, too dirty to allow its logo to be read, sat peak-backward on top of his head. Tufts of blond hair stuck out the bottom of the hat. The envelope in his hand obviously did not contain an application for anyone's secretarial pool.

Jack reflected on his own youthful job searches as he drove away on his next errand.

Monica Ferris was a large girl, with bad hair, and thick glasses. She was dressed the part of a secretary, but seemed out of place in the corporate office of a national trucking firm. Jack arranged to speak to her during the lunch hour.

They sat at her desk, while she ate her tuna fish sandwich and sipped her diet Coke.

"I understand that you were friends with Rhonda Fuku-shima. Jimmie Heddon gave me your name," Jack began.

Her eyes began to tear up, and her jaw began to quiver, as she tried to answer.

"It was so sad. One day we were laughing, and joking, and talking about our futures, and the next I hear, she's gone. She was such a good friend to me."

"I've very sorry for your loss," Jack said. "Forgive me, but I need to ask you some questions. It could go a long way to finding out who killed your friend.

"How did she and Jimmie get along? Did you notice? Did she ever say anything?"

"They seemed to get along just fine," the girl replied. "I'd say that she liked him a lot. I mean, she was carrying his baby and all. Course, I don't know what they were like when they were alone. I guess they got along.

"Her dad didn't like him. At least, that's what Ronnie told me. He used to yell at her. And I think he threatened to break them up one time. Ronnie used to cry a lot when she talked about how her father hated Jimmie. She wanted, so much, for her dad to like him."

"How did Jimmie feel about her being pregnant?"

"I never talked to him about stuff like that, but Ronnie told me that he was sort of okay with it. I mean, neither one of them wanted to be tied down, right now, but they had done what they did, and Jimmie was going to make things right."

"They were going to get married?"

"Yep. I don't think they had set a date. Ronnie was trying to figure out how she was going to tell her parents, first."

"Did they ever have fights or disagreements?" Jack listened carefully.

"Oh yeah. They had their moments. They'd argue, usually about dumb stuff, like what kind of beer to buy, or where to go for dinner. Like I said, when they were alone, who knows what went on?"

"Did they ever get into a fight over anything else—apart from the regular things folks might disagree about?"

"Well, they seemed to have a lot of yelling matches about her parents. He thought they were too controlling. She always felt she owed them some respect.

"They were very 'Old World,' in Jimmie's opinion, and Rhonda was convinced they would change. She objected when he would be unkind about her parents' traditional views."

"So Rhonda agreed with her parents?"

"That would be stretching it, I think. She was North American to the bone, but protected her parents' right to hold the views they did. She and Jimmie argued most after her father had got all angry about her hanging with folks from another culture. But, they loved each other. I think Jimmie would have done anything for her." Monica took the last bite of her sandwich, and washed it down with the diet pop.

"So you would say Jimmie isn't likely the one responsible for her death?"

"Are you kidding? He's the last one I'd believe had anything to do with it."

"Interesting. Someone else I spoke to figures Jimmie is responsible."

"Well they are wrong." She pounded a fist for emphasis. Her empty pop can shook.

"Can you think of anyone who might have done this to your friend?" Jack leaned closer. Monica fixed her eyes on his.

"I can't think of a soul," she said.

"Any idea why she would end up in an office in the middle of town, in the evening, like she did?"

"Oh, that's easy. She had a job interview."

Jack checked to see his jaw hadn't dropped too far.

"With who?" His eyebrows almost disappeared into his hairline.

"A Mr. Biggs, I think she said. She was quite excited about it, I remember."

"She had applied for a job at Biggs, Wilberforce, Hutton, and Small?" Jack asked.

"Is that the name of the place? No, she was a NIP, like me?"

"I beg your pardon?"

"A Northern Inter-City Placement; a NIP. We were both registered at the same place. That's how I ended up here to-day. I don't think this one is permanent, though."

"Rhonda had been offered a permanent job?"

"Yeah. That's what I gather. That's why she was so excited."

"Northern Inter-City Placements called her up and told her Biggs, Wilberforce, Hutton, and Small had a permanent position?" Jack began to worry for his friend, again.

"Well, no. That was the strange thing. She got this call from the company directly. They left a message for her to come to the office that night."

"Who called her?"

"I don't know. All I know is that she said she was going up there and was going to meet a guy for the interview."

"Does the placement office ever have an employer call an applicant?"

"That's a strange thing too. They never give out that kind of information, in case we go to the place and don't like it, or we don't work out. That way the employer has to call NIP to complain, or get a replacement. No way they should have given out Rhonda's number."

Where to start first? Jack wondered. This girl had given him some brand new riddles to solve. He was getting desperate for answers. At least he had a reason for Rhonda to have been in Brendan Biggs' office. But Brendan might have to answer some questions before all this was over.

"Thank you so much. You have been a great help to me. I hope I'll be able to find the person who killed your friend," Jack said, with more conviction in his voice than in his heart.

Monica's eyes teared up again. "I hope so too. I'm going to miss her so much."

"Keep watching the papers. Have a good afternoon."

"Thanks," she said as she folded up the wrappings of her lunch, picked up the empty can, and returned them to the paper bag in which she had brought them.

Jack backtracked to the placement office. He needed to find out how Rhonda's name and number had come to be given out to Biggs, Wilberforce, Hutton, and Small. And he wondered who it was that had asked for her. He was afraid someone else was going to mention Brendan Biggs and the murdered girl in the same sentence, again. The idea of a cell phone was appealing more and more as he watched his odometer flip over the numbers while he drove through the early afternoon traffic.

Chapter Twenty-two

Back at Northern Inter-City Placements, another group of hopeful unemployed was waiting for interviews. It seemed to Jack that some of the new crowd were not so young. As the day drew to a close, people who had been hunting on their own became more open to the idea of placing their name on a list and accepting whatever job might come open for them. They were far less choosy than they had been earlier in the day.

Jack waited for the woman at the desk to have a free moment before approaching her to ask the questions his interview with Monica had raised.

He identified himself to her again, but this time added that he was working with the police to try to solve the murder of Rhonda Fukushima.

That wasn't exactly the truth. The police knew he was looking for answers, the same as they were. Certainly Brown and Willis did. Valerie did too. But he had no standing with the police. What the lady at the desk didn't know wouldn't hurt anyone, he supposed, unless he was found out.

"I'm trying to track down the name of the individual who

called offering a job at Biggs, Wilberforce, Hutton, and Small Advertising Agency a couple of weeks ago. Apparently they were given Ms. Fukushima's name and number, and made contact with her directly."

"Oh, I don't think that is possible, Mr. Elton," the woman said. "We would never give out information like that." She went on to repeat essentially what Monica had said about insulating applicants from the employers so that the agency could handle complaints, or replacements.

"Of course, if an applicant works out for an employer, they would give all that information to the employer, themselves, and we would drop out of the loop. For the first contact, though, we would make all the arrangements here."

"So, you would never make a recommendation, by name, to someone who called you looking for a temporary or part-time worker?" Jack asked.

"It would be highly unusual. Let me see what I can find for you."

She typed some information into her computer and waited while it searched the database. She looked over the top of her glasses as she stabbed at the cursor keys to get at just the right place on her screen.

"Well, there she is, in the file. There is a list of the places we have referred her to. What did you say was the name of the firm that was hiring?"

"Biggs, Wilberforce, Hutton, and Small," said Jack.

"Let's see. No, that's not it. Um, how about this one. Nope." She looked up at Jack. "According to what I have here, we never referred her to such a place."

Jack's heart sank at this revelation. Who at Brendan's office would have wanted to hire a young woman, and how did they get the information, without going through the proper procedures?

"Could you look up Biggs, Wilberforce, Hutton, and Small, in your computer, and see which job openings they have posted? Maybe I can get at it from that angle."

"Just a moment." The woman's fingers flew over the keyboard again. The same rapid tapping of the arrow keys. The myopic stare at the screen.

"I'm sorry to tell you, that company does not do business with us. We have no listings, at all, under that name. I'm afraid you are going to have to look somewhere else for your information."

Jack left the placement office, feeling totally let down. He would check with someone in personnel at Brendan's workplace. He hoped he would not hit a dead end there too. This was becoming more complicated than he had initially thought.

Jack drove to the office tower housing the advertising firm and went to the eleventh floor. An older man in the personnel department welcomed him into his cubicle and introduced himself, thrusting out his hand in greeting.

"I'm Trevor Munro, Mr. Elton. How can I be of assistance? I understand you are working to try to get Mr. Biggs off the suspect list for that rather unhappy incident in the office."

"Yes. I was wondering if you could tell me what openings you were trying to fill, around the time of the murder, that would have brought the girl in here for an interview."

"The answer to that question is easy. There were none."

"You have not been looking to fill any positions lately?"

"No, Mr. Elton. We have our full complement of staff and, with the economy the way it is, we have no view to hiring for the foreseeable future. You see, we are a company that has to maintain a high level of quality in the work we produce. We scout in the schools and colleges to fill our ranks. We do not ordinarily advertise for positions, but rather, recruit graduates based on their marks and the type of work they are producing. We would not invite a girl to come in for an interview in the office. We usually do our recruiting interviews where the candidates are studying. It's more cost effective."

"So, it would be impossible that she would be called in to fill an office position—secretary, receptionist, or whatever?"

"Extremely unusual. We go to the secretarial schools and technical colleges for those types of jobs. We require people who are well trained in computers and can handle word processing, spreadsheets, databases—that sort of thing."

"Where would someone get the idea that you wanted to hire for a permanent position, then?"

"I have no idea. I'm sorry I haven't been much help." Trevor Munro looked genuinely regretful.

"Well, you've closed some doors. But others are opening. Thanks for your time."

Jack dropped into Brendan's office, only briefly, to say hello, and to bring him up to date on what had been happening.

Brendan was understandably distressed.

"Do things always move this slowly, in an investigation of this sort?" he asked.

"Not always, but sometimes it takes a little longer. Of course, when you are under suspicion as the perpetrator, I would imagine that it feels like an eternity, no matter how quickly things are resolved.

"The police want to get this sorted out as quickly as possible too. With each passing minute, the trail gets a little colder, and the resolution becomes more difficult."

Brendan heard Jack out about the job offer that Rhonda had apparently received.

"Jack, that's just crazy. We don't—we can't—operate like that, and still claim to be professionals. There is absolutely no chance that anyone from Biggs, Wilberforce, Hutton, and Small would go outside the regular chain of command to hire someone. If they did, we'd be scouting the schools to find a replacement for the renegade employee."

"That's exactly what your guy in personnel said before I came to see you. All I can do, now, is promise to get back to you when I finally get some new information."

"Believe me, Jack. If I find anything that will help to get me out of this spotlight, you'll be the first person I call."

Jack had one more stop to make before his to-do list was completed for the day.

Chapter Twenty-three

J ack's investigations, today, had gleaned the most information so far, but had also raised the most questions. He couldn't remember. Did Rhonda live with her parents? Maybe they knew something about the message she received. Fukushima's was just around the corner, and down the block, from Brendan's office. Jack had decided to take a late afternoon stroll to see if the girl's father might be able to shed a little more light on the subject.

The sandwich board on the sidewalk directed Jack, once again, to the little shop where the tourists stopped on their way to, or from, the bigger attractions of the city.

As he entered the store, he noticed that there was someone else helping the customers this particular afternoon; a short, plump lady, with almond eyes, black hair, and wearing a floral print dress. She walked as if in constant pain. It was a sort of shuffle, as though she was afraid to lift her feet. She would often support herself on the shelving as she tried her best to keep up with the clientèle.

Jack waited his turn.

"May I help you?" The woman looked up at Jack, with dark eyes, and a trace of sadness.

"I was hoping to find Mr. Fukushima here. Is he around this afternoon?"

"I'm sorry. He's not here right now. He is over making arrangements for a funeral. Our daughter died, and now we have to bury her. I am Mrs. Fukushima."

"I'm so sorry to hear of your loss. I am Jack Elton. I'm trying to find out who might have killed your daughter."

The woman stood with eyes downcast. "That is something most distressing. My daughter was a good girl. She never had any trouble. She was obedient and honorable."

There may have been some things you didn't know.

"Did she seem worried lately?" he asked.

"No. Very happy all the time. Never seemed to worry."

"Did she tell you she was looking for a full-time job?"

"Yes. She was very happy on the day she died." The mother's eyes began to mist over. She blinked the tears away and continued. "She received a message that a man wanted to see her for a job—full-time. At a big office, downtown here. She would have been close to us."

"Was she living with you and Mr. Fukushima?"

"Oh, yes. Very good girl. Not like some, who leave their parents, and start to run around with the wrong crowd."

"So, this person called your house to make the appointment?"

"That is what happened. Rhonda told me that. She was to go to the big advertising company at night, and talk to a man there."

"Did she know the man's name?"

"She said she was going to see a Mr. Biggs."

Jack suddenly had a sour taste in his mouth. He was almost certain that Brendan had not invited the girl to his office that night. If that was true, the only other explanation was that someone had been impersonating him. That person was the killer. But all that the police were going to care about was that Brendan was implicated by the testimony of the friends and parents.

"Are you sure it was Mr. Biggs who called?"

"Yes, quite sure. She showed me a note with his name on it."

"Did she write the note? Did she talk to Mr. Biggs on the phone?"

The woman shook her head, as if trying to recall. A blank look indicated, to Jack, that it was unlikely that Rhonda's mother knew anything for sure.

"I guess. I don't know how she heard from him. But, she had that note, saying when and where to go. It said to see Mr. Biggs."

Jack wasn't at all sure that the woman understood the importance of his question. He decided to let the subject drop for the time being. He hoped that, when Mr. Fukushima had had time to get over his grief, he might be able to provide a little more detail, as well.

"Thank you ma'am. Please let your husband know I was here. I will be in to see him later in the week, if that is all right. Again, my sympathies over your loss."

"You are welcome, sir." The little lady gave a bow, which Jack returned, as best he could; before fleeing back to the sidewalk.

In the stop-and-go of the afternoon parade, Jack reflected on the past few days. He figured that he would spend the evening piecing together as much as he could, and then making his plans about where he might go from there. He realized that he was making an assumption by theorizing that there was actually some place to go from where he found himself in his investigation.

Ordinarily, he would have been frustrated by the slow traffic, but the mental process he was going through only seemed to be enhanced by the mindless rhythm of gas and brake, gas and brake. Soon he was outside his building. He parked and went up to his apartment.

The stairs were narrow and dimly lit. Today, it seemed the smell of cleaning fluid and old clothing from the thrift shop on the main floor was more intense than usual. The stairs creaked as he went. He dug in his pocket for his keys.

Once inside the apartment, he threw down his coat on a chair and put the keys on a small table by the door where he would be sure to find them.

Jack went to the cupboard and stared blankly at the row of cans, deciding what special treat he might prepare for tonight. It was a toss-up between tomato soup and Spaghetti-O's. He chose the latter, reasoning that, since he had missed lunch again, he could use the extra bulk of a few limp noodles. A plate of toast would be a good complement to the meal, along with a half bottle of the house orange juice.

He didn't start the meal right way. He had a phone call to make, first.

"Hiya. How was your day?" he asked.

"Hectic," Valerie Cummins said. "I had to deal with some folks who seemed to have great difficulty understanding that it's illegal to travel over the speed limit, even if you're late for an appointment. They didn't take kindly to my suggestion that, since I had stopped them, they might at least arrive alive. They were just ticked that they would arrive late.

"Quite a choice to have to make," she continued. "Which

is preferable, late and alive or on time and dead? Let me think about that.

"Later in the day, I could have shown them which was better. We responded to the scene of an accident where only two of the five people involved would end up anywhere alive.

Jack filled Valerie in on his quest for answers including the revelation that somehow Rhonda Fukushima had been summoned to the offices of Biggs, Wilberforce, Hutton, and Small by persons as yet unknown.

"Any ideas about where I might go from here? I need a fresh perspective on this thing," he asked.

"I think you need to speak to some more of her friends. See what they know. Sometimes the smallest little detail will be the key to the whole thing. Use that list that Jimmie gave you. Maybe chase him down at work with this new information and see if he can think of anything new to add. Of course, there's always the chance that he knows more than he's letting on. He strikes me as a smooth talker. He was able to talk Rhonda into the sack."

"I know you're right," Jack said. "It's just that I've run into so many stumbling blocks lately, I'm almost afraid to try to go any deeper, 'cause I'm afraid I'll just end up with more questions."

Valerie changed the subject. "When are we going out again?"

"You are certainly very forward, young lady."

"The clock's a-tickin.' If I waited for guys to invite me out, I'd be an old maid and would starve to death to boot. This is a new age, mister. Women are going to take over. Now, when are you going to invite me out to a no-strings-attached dinner for two?"

"No strings attached, eh?"

"I meant that payback would not involve sitting in on the

interrogation of someone you had a professional interest in. I'll be nice to you if you'll be nice to me, if you get my drift."

Jack caught her drift, and dearly wished that he didn't feel snowed under by the work he had to do.

"Not tonight, unfortunately. How about we set a date for this weekend? We'll go out to that little place on the harbor I was telling you about. It'll be fun, and I won't have this business on my mind, I promise."

Valerie agreed that that would be something to look forward to. She would not be working on the weekend and could give her complete attention to him. They decided on Saturday evening. He would pick her up at six o'clock.

"Now, that doesn't mean you can't call me, or see me, on the other days, you know. We can go for coffee."

"And donuts," Jack added with a laugh.

"That's a bad stereotype. If you want to really get on my bad side, just keep that up." She chuckled.

"Oh, I'm sorry officer. I was mistaken."

"That's better. I like the ones with the white icing and the colored sprinkles, by the way."

They both laughed. Jack said he would be in touch, and hung up. The day was not a total loss, after all.

Chapter Twenty-four

After his meal of tinned pasta and toast, Jack sat down with pencil and paper and began to consolidate his information; the little notes that he had made to himself on bits of scrap paper, as well as stuff he had crammed into his head over the past few days.

What could be the motive for such a murder? Who was the person who had left the message? These were the questions that had to be answered. They were the key. Jack was convinced that the answers would be as intriguing as everything that had gone before, and then some.

He looked over the list that he had been given by Jimmie Heddon, and decided to take it to Chief Detective Brown. Perhaps the police could tell Jack if any of Jimmie's and Rhonda's acquaintances had a criminal record. At this point it didn't matter who finally found the answers. The police were the ones who would make the final decisions about who to arrest. Jack was just trying to help the process along.

He spent the rest of the evening lying on the couch with the television on. The programs included a couple of police dramas and a reality show where a girl had to choose a possible husband from a group of twenty-five, one of whom was a millionaire. Jack saw none of them. He woke up after the late news was over, turned off the TV, and fell into bed.

He was up early the next morning, preparing for his visit to the police department and his interview of another of Rhonda's friends.

The day was dull and gray. It was a perfect match to Jack's mood. He was beginning to feel as though all his efforts were only reinforcing the suspicions the police had about Brendan's guilt. Rhonda's friends were all in agreement that Biggs was the man she had been going to see. Her parents, or at least her mother, said she had heard Rhonda was going to see Biggs. Was it worth the risk of hearing the same all over again? Maybe today would be different. He doubted it.

The drive along rain-soaked streets did nothing to lift Jack's depression. Apparently others were upset by the change in the weather as well. Horns blared, and road rage was much in evidence, as the impatient jockeyed to get to the next red light more quickly than their fellow travelers.

Images of the same wet streets on the morning that started this most recent quest resurfaced in Jack's mind. He could almost feel the party headache he had had that morning resurfacing. Probably the tension of driving in today's rush hour, he supposed. He remembered driving up the hill, and passing Brendan's office that day, unaware that there was a dead body in the office complex on the eleventh floor. He remembered Gregory Fukushima out on the sidewalk getting ready for the day's commerce.

Jack sat up suddenly in the driver's seat, nearly driving his head through the ceiling liner. Until now, he had not been able to make out who the man on the sidewalk was. The flashback in the rain had made the face clear in his mind. It had been Rhonda's father who he had seen as he drove up the hill past the bus terminal from the party. *Poor guy, he had no idea what that day was going to hold, and how his life was going to be changed forever.*

He parked in the visitors' lot outside the police station again and walked through the rain, hunched over, with his jacket over his head. Once inside, he sought out the men's room before approaching the gatekeeper behind the glass partition.

He worked the crank on the paper towel machine until he had a large enough strip to dry himself, before heading out to the desk to seek admission. He was thankful, as he combed his hair in front of the mirror, that the police department was not so modern as to have air dryers. He always felt a little foolish trying to get dry in front of one of those things after coming in out of the rain.

The officer at the desk buzzed Jack through the door, once he had convinced her that he had business on the other side.

He went straight to Brown's office, and found his friend filling in forms.

"What have we got here?" he asked.

"Standard operating procedure. We've got a drug case to finish up. The paperwork takes more time than the bust, and it's got to be done right. They never show that on TV, you know. What's up with you?"

"I was going to ask you to do some checks for me, but I've thought better of it seeing as you have other things on your mind." Jack folded his list and stuffed it into his coat pocket.

"Thanks for your consideration. I'm afraid that I wouldn't be able to do much for you right now anyway. If you get something that really needs to be done, let me know. I'll try to fit it in. This wasn't a suspect, or anything, was it?" The detective checked a box on the form he was filling, and made a hasty note on one of the lines.

"No. Just trying to narrow the field, in case someone had a criminal background. You got anything new on our girl?"

"No. Nothing new. Nothing planned. We've got other things right now. We haven't dropped the investigation. It's just not a top priority at the moment."

"Where is Biggs in your plan? I mean, is he still your prime suspect, or what?" Jack pulled up a chair and sat.

"Barring anything else, he's our only suspect. Mind you, I think we'd have a hard time making a court case," the detective added. "All we have now is that note Larry Walle found. I'm not at all sure that is sufficient motivation for an all-out prosecution. It's just his name and address and a time."

"Yeah, about that note." Jack waited for the detective to finish a comment he was writing on his form.

The detective put down his pen and looked across his desk. "Go on."

"There are some strange goings-on surrounding how she got that information."

"You don't say." Brown raised an eyebrow.

"The story is that someone called her home saying they were Brendan Biggs, or representing him; I'm not sure which yet. This person said they had a permanent job for Rhonda at Biggs, Wilberforce, Hutton, and Small."

"And your point is?" The detective scratched his head, and raised the other eyebrow.

"She had not applied to the company for work. She worked though a placement agency, and they never give out personal information to potential employers."

"You're suggesting that there is something fishy going on?"

"I'm thinking that someone might have wanted to lure her into the office for some reason. Maybe the intention was murder. Maybe not. But, while she was there, she met whoever it was and, as a result of whatever transpired, ended up dead."

"It doesn't look any better for Biggs," Brown suggested.

"I suppose not, but unless you can show that the murder occurred at a time other than the one Dr. Walle gives, you don't really have a case. You saw the video."

"Well, like I said, it's dropped in priority, not because it isn't an important case, but because we just don't have a clear direction to go at present. Now, if you were to come in here with the name of a suspect that we could interrogate, I can assure you that the case would be bumped up to a higher level."

"I'll certainly keep my eyes and ears open, but I don't have all the resources at my disposal that you do."

"Ah, but I understand that you are gaining the attention of one of our younger members." The detective gave a broad smile.

"The grapevine sure seems to work well around here." Jack could feel his face growing hot.

"Next time you're out in the parking lot, have a look at our security system. We scan that area looking for unsavory types. You and Officer Cummins were the subject of some close scrutiny the other day. That's how the rumors got started." Another grin, accompanied by an exaggerated wink.

"Is Dr. Walle down in his dungeon?" Jack went for a change of subject.

"Not sure, but if you don't mind walking around among dead people, you are most welcome to go down there and look for him. He'll be the one who is upright and breathing."

"Thanks. I'm sure he'll be easy to spot." Jack stood up and replaced the chair in its original location.

The two men said their good-byes. Jack headed out to look for the coroner. The detective was hunched over his desk, laboring over his forms, again.

When Jack arrived at the foot of the stairs, he pressed the button that operated the doors and they swung in with their usual sigh. When he walked into the morgue, it was apparent that the night before had been a busy one. Six draped gurneys were lined up along the corridor leading to the autopsy lab.

Dr. Lawrence Walle was hovering over yet another body on his steel table. The subject of the doctor's interest had already had his chest laid open in the typical fashion of autopsies. A surgical towel covered the man's face. Another, over his genitals, preserved what little dignity was left. Jack was careful to keep at a safe distance, across the room by the door, in case a fast retreat was necessitated.

The coroner looked up. "You should consider yourself very fortunate. Not everyone is allowed down here during working hours."

"I have friends in higher places," Jack said with a smile and a nod of the head, indicating the next floor up.

"I suppose you want to pick my brain some more about that girl from the office tower?" The doctor hefted a liver, and placed it in a hanging scale basket. He watched the needle settle on the scale, and looked through the bottom of his bifocals. He stepped on the foot operated recorder switch, and made a verbal record of the weight.

"Yes, I did have one question for you."

"I hope I can answer it from memory. As you might have noticed, we've got a lot of work to do today. A couple of homicides and a horrendous three-vehicle accident on the highway."

"What can you tell me about the knife that was used in the

stabbing?" Jack looked away as the doctor delved deeper into the abdominal cavity of his latest client.

"I'm not sure what that information will do for you. It's usually the detectives who want that sort of stuff so they can look for weapons. But I can tell you, without having to look at my notes. Actually it's a very interesting subject." He placed a kidney in the scale.

"Can you tell me about it?"

"The implement used was a narrow blade. I'd have to say that it was no more than three-quarters of an inch wide at the hilt. Marks on the body indicate that it was some sort of folding blade. The point was sharp but the blade itself appears to have had a relatively dull edge, perhaps from use. The wounds showed signs of tearing as opposed to the sort of cutting you might see with a sharper implement."

"How long would you say this thing was?" The doctor had taken another sample from the abdomen, and was recording his findings on the tape.

Walle lifted his toe from the switch on the floor.

"I would say not longer than three and a half inches from the tip to the handle. It probably had a handle in proportion to its length. That would add three and a half to four inches. I would place the total length of the weapon at around seven and a half inches."

Jack's brow furrowed. "Who would have a knife like that?"

"Doesn't have to be a knife. But, it could be. It could have been designed for something else, perhaps a fancy letter opener. Could be a common pen knife that's been changed through use and just looks like something it isn't. It's one of those things you know after you find the suspected weapon. If I had more free time, I could do a more detailed analysis, but just look around." The doctor glanced over his shoulder at the line of steel stretchers awaiting his attention. He closed the chest flaps with bloodied hands and stripped off his rubber gloves.

"I'm afraid that's the best I can do at the moment," the coroner continued. "I'm kind of busy right now." He washed and dried his hands before donning a clean pair of rubber gloves and starting to thread a semi-circular needle with heavy suture.

"Well, thank you, doctor. I'm not sure how I'll use that information yet, but you never can tell how these things will add up. I'll let you get back to your work. Thank you." Jack turned for the door.

"Not a problem. I wish I had more time." There was a trace of sadness in his voice as he picked up the suture, and began a rough repair of the Y-incision.

Chapter Twenty-five

Jack walked back up the stairs to the first floor. He had hoped that he might see Valerie coming or going this morning, but all the officers were out on their patrols by the time he concluded his meeting with the coroner. He headed out to his car, patting his pockets to locate the list of Rhonda Fukushima's friends that Jimmie Heddon had given him.

One address was in an area of town that was familiar to Jack. He chose to go in that direction.

The skies were clearing as he left the parking lot and headed north of the city. The trip would take him about thirty-five minutes, depending on the traffic. The countryside helped to clear his mind of some of the sights he had seen in Dr. Walle's morgue.

The young woman on his list worked out of her home, according to a note Jimmie had added to the list. The address was on a quiet rural road past fields of corn and cabbages. The air was alternately sweet with the smell of hay, and ripe with the odors of cattle and pig farms still struggling to keep the ever-expanding city at a distance.

Memories of the early days of his youth flooded Jack's mind. He thought of the summers that he had spent with his family on his uncle's farm. Though the recollections were more than thirty years old, they still came into clear focus in his mind. Life was simpler back then, not just for Jack but for most folks.

It was an era when technology had not yet begun to encroach on human creativity and resourcefulness. It was, he thought, a time when neighbors shared closer ties with one another, and when disagreements were resolved by simpler means. He reflected on the possibility that it might have been a time when someone like Rhonda would not have been killed over a disagreement, if disagreement had indeed been what led to her fatal encounter.

Jack returned from his reverie, and pulled in at the mailbox marked Cripps. There was also a sign that read Cripps Financial Services - Typing Service. A long gravel road led back from the main road to a two-story, wood-framed, house with a separate garage at the end of the drive. There had probably been a barn out back, at one time, Jack supposed, but not any more.

A bicycle leaned against the side of the building. The grass looked like it needed cutting. The front porch creaked ominously as he stepped up to the front door. He knocked tentatively.

A voice from inside called out, "C'mon in. It isn't locked. Take off your shoes. I just did the floor."

Jack entered the home cautiously, not wanting to surprise anyone.

Though the place had obviously gone through some renovations in the past, there was no hiding the fact that this had once been the home of a farmer.

The kitchen was enormous. A small table with four chairs looked out of place in the center of the room. It made the area look larger still.

Jack could imagine the large family dining set that would have occupied the space years ago. Unlike more modern kitchens, this one had a couch sitting against one wall. Its design, and the well-worn cushions, spoke of a long history, and vigorous use. Children's books littered the floor in front of the ancient piece of furniture.

A modern, gas-fueled stove sat towards the back of the kitchen, against the wall where, Jack estimated, a cast-iron, wood-burning stove had once been. A circular metal plate was affixed over a spot on the wall where the stovepipe would have passed through to the outside. The plate had been painted many times by the look of it.

The kitchen sink stood under a window that gave a view of the field to the far side of the house. From the pile of dishes, Jack was certain that no one had been looking out that window at length for quite some time. A neat row of shoes stood by the door. The green-and-white-tiled floor was clean. The air smelled of bleach mixed with the telltale odor of unwashed dishes.

He closed the door, took off his own shoes, and added them to the rest of the footwear. Then he gently tapped on the counter, to let the owner of the voice know he had complied with the order to enter.

"For heavens sake man quit that racket. I'm a-comin', what on earth do you want this time?"

Jack looked up to see the largest, roundest woman he had seen in a long time. She was the color of semi-sweet chocolate and, with about a hundred and fifty fewer pounds, might have been considered attractive.

"Oh my, oh my. You aren't who I was expecting to see out here. I was expecting someone else. Who are you? And what do you want?" Anger and fear mixed on her face. Her wide eyes stared at Jack, and her hands rested on her hips. She cocked her head to one side, waiting for an answer.

"My name is Jack Elton. I'm working with the police to try to solve the murder of Rhonda Fukushima."

There was that little lie again about working with the police. It seemed necessary due to his uncertainty about whether the woman meant him any harm.

When she heard her friend's name, though, her expression softened and her muscles relaxed. Jack relaxed a little too.

He learned that Nondice Cripps had met Rhonda when they were attending secretarial college together. Rhonda had not applied herself fully, and never received her certificate. Nondice, on the other hand, had completed the course, and gone into business for herself when she could not get a job at the numerous companies to which she delivered her resume.

Jack stood, listening quietly, as Nondice poured out all this information. It was as if she were trying to justify her present standard of living, and to verify her friendship with the dead woman.

"I got a little boy. His daddy left me just after he was born. It's a good thing I have the business. Otherwise I'd never survive. I do some accounting for the farmers in the area, and for my church. It doesn't bring in a lot of money. I do typing for folks, as well. Sometimes they bring me stuff to copy. Other times they just tell me what they want, and I do it for them. I get by. I'll be able to take care of my boy until I find a caring man."

"I understand that you were talking to Rhonda the week before she died."

Jack felt the pressure to get on with his business. He was feeling a little uncomfortable being alone in this house with an unattached woman, even though she was clearly not his type. Valerie would have been another matter, but he put that thought out of his mind, for the time being.

The woman dragged a wooden chair from under the table, and settled into it. She motioned for Jack to sit on the couch. He moved some of the juvenile reading materials and sat.

"Yeah, we were out together, some of us girls," Nondice said. "I was able to get someone to baby-sit little Jeremy. You don't know how tough it is to get good help for baby-sitting. I've had some girls come in who just talk on the phone all night, or watch TV, and poor little Jeremy, why he's—"

"What sorts of things did you talk about, if I may ask?"

"Oh, you know, girl stuff. Babies, boyfriends, or the absence of boyfriends. Rhonda was telling us about her and Jimmie Heddon, and how they were planning to get married. She was going to have his baby. She hadn't told her parents. She was afraid they'd get angry. She was a little frantic about that."

"How do you mean, frantic?"

"Mister, her parents were as old school as they come. They probably would have forced her into an arranged marriage, if it hadn't been declared illegal in this country.

"There was stuff young girls did, and stuff they didn't even think about, and Mr. F was as rigid as a fence post about that. When she finally got around to telling him she was in a family way, I suspect there was going to be a lot of heat generated. Rhonda wanted our advice about how to bring the subject up. I think we all agreed it was going to be a tough call.

"She was worried about raising the kid too. She was sure her parents wouldn't be of much help, but she'd been looking for work."

"I'd be interested to know if she mentioned anything to you about a job interview she was going to have," Jack said.

"Did she? You could hardly shut her up about it. She had this opportunity to work full-time for a big wig advertising executive downtown. She had got this message. They called her directly. Imagine that. She was going to see this guy, Briggs or Boggs or something like that."

"You say they called her directly. Do you know if she spoke to this person herself?"

"It was during the day. She wouldn't have been home. I remember her saying that her father gave her the message that the call had come in for her. Does it really make a difference?"

"It might. Do you know of anyone that might have wanted to hurt her?"

"Can't think of a one," Nondice replied. "Everybody loved Rhonda."

"Somebody didn't," Jack said.

Nondice just stared back.

Jack thanked her for the information she had been able to offer and prepared to head back to town.

"I sure hope you find out who killed my friend. Whoever it was is just plain evil, by my way of thinking." A large tear coursed down the side of Nondice's round face. Others waited their turn in each eye.

"I'm certainly going to do everything I can to track that person down," Jack said. He did not care to mention the fact that he had a friend who had been attacked, in a different way, by Rhonda's killer.

He thanked Nondice again, as he tied on his shoes at the door. The two shook hands, and he headed to his car.

Taken separately, the pieces meant nothing. The stories all seemed the same but there were subtle nuances that, taken together, were beginning to lead him in a different direction for the solution to the murder, and the complete absolution of his friend.

Jack's concentration was broken on the outskirts of town by the sight of red and blue flashing lights in his rearview mirror. He obediently pulled over and dug his license out of his pocket. He opened the glove compartment to get the registration.

The voice at the window said, "Okay pardner, where's the fire?"

He grinned and answered, "In your eyes, Officer Cummins."

"You were going too fast there. Don't let yourself get distracted. I've got a job to do, friend or not. And I've got a personal stake in your safety. Haven't you been listening to my horror stories about some of the accidents that I have had to attend? Consider this a warning. Have a safe afternoon, sir. Give me a call tonight."

Valerie handed the license and registration papers back through the window and walked back to her cruiser. She made a note in her record book, and started the powerful engine of the patrol car. She flashed Jack a smile as she powered away past him.

He put his wallet away and resumed his journey at a more

reasonable pace. He had to admit that he was shaking a little from the encounter, even if the officer was the love of his life. There had been a look on Valerie's face that convinced him that she cared—and that she meant business.

Chapter Twenty-six

Jack headed back to the police station. Ordinarily the backtracking would have been an annoyance to him. He liked a little order to his life, and the constant back and forth of the last few days had not been a pleasant experience. This time, however, he was on a quest for important information. He wanted to get some facts straight. The input from one of his old friends might confirm his suspicions. Perhaps the day that began on such a negative note would end with him on the way to solving a crime.

He made his inquiry and was ushered into an office.

The two men talked for over an hour. Jack asked his questions and wrote down the answers. He shared the information he had gleaned, from friends and family members, and listened intently as his friend gave an opinion.

Jack emerged from the meeting, surprised by what he had discovered, and startled by what he now suspected. He turned back to the officer with whom he had been speaking.

"And you're confident that this is worth pursuing? I find

it hard to believe that what you've told me could be possible."

The man gave a solemn nod.

The lack of concrete information and solid evidence was still disconcerting. Apart from Jimmie and Nondice, there was no one who seemed able to add anything that Jack had not already heard.

"What would you do in a situation like this?"

Jack was standing in Chief Detective Brown's office, now. Keegan Willis had gone home at the end of his shift. Jack considered himself fortunate to have found Brown still at work, and by himself.

"Jack, this is the stuff that frustrates the police more than anything else. It's what makes for a 'cold case.' It sure would be nice to have evidence just drop into your lap all the time, but it's not reality. We've got more resources than you, and you can see where we are. The girl's murder has dropped in priority precisely because we have no leads—no place to go.

"Believe me," the detective continued. "I'd love to be able to sew this case up tight. I think her parents deserve to have some closure. Comfort will have to wait till later, no matter what we do."

"At first, I just wanted to clear Brendan Biggs," Jack said. "Now I've become so involved, and incensed, that I just feel the need to try and find the perpetrator."

"Just remember, Jack, you're not a cop anymore. Don't pretend that you are. I still believe in you, but there are plenty of others who have bought the story that got you fired."

"Thanks for your support," Jack replied.

"Let me know if you have any more luck than we're

having. And believe me, at this point, all we have is luck to go on.

This is not a contest, Jack thought, as he left the building. *Whoever can solve the puzzle first, will have done a service to society, and will gain a little justice for Rhonda Fukushima.*

He pulled out of the parking lot, and headed into afternoon traffic. He had one more visit to make.

His next stop was at the Fukushimas' little shop. There were some details he needed to verify there too. As he entered he could see that as on his previous visits, the person at the counter was occupied with customers. It was Mrs. Fukushima who was taking care of the shop this afternoon.

While he waited, Jack looked around the store at some of the merchandise. Besides dealing in souvenirs, the Fukushimas imported trinkets from China and Japan. These were displayed on one side of the shop, on brightly lit shelves. Jack examined Chinese fans and small works in jade. There were various sized glass boxes and candle holders, and children's toys of different kinds, both battery-powered and wind-up. One shelf held blank notebooks with colorful printed covers, made in China. He looked over the inventory with interest.

The sound of shuffling feet behind him alerted Jack to the approach of Mrs. Fukushima. When he turned she was standing behind him, her brow deeply wrinkled with concern. There was no welcoming smile.

"I remember you. You are that man with the police. Do you know who killed my daughter?"

"Good afternoon ma'am. I think I'm getting closer to an answer. Is your husband in today?"

Her expression turned to one of profound sadness. Her tear-filled eyes were downcast. A single drop coursed down each round cheek.

"Tomorrow is the service for my daughter. He is making the final arrangements at Les Sables Funeral Home. It is to be a traditional service. There is much planning. We will be closed for the next two days."

"I see. I had hoped to ask him a question or two. Will he be here next week?"

"Oh yes. That is certain. I have to be away next week. He will have to take care of the shop."

"Well, I won't bother you any more during what I am sure must be a very sad time. Might I use your phone before I go?"

"Oh, no. We don't have a phone here. My husband does not like using the phone. It disturbs his business. We only have a phone at home. I'm so sorry."

"That won't be a problem. I can call from someplace else. Thank you for your time."

Jack headed out again. The tide was turning. He felt that he was getting closer all the time. Just a few more answers would confirm the direction he would need to go in the investigation. He hoped to have something concrete to share with the police, Brendan Biggs, and all those concerned about Rhonda, very soon.

He found a pay phone, and dialed the number he had written down. There was no answer. He walked back to where he had left his car.

It was Friday, and it was late in the afternoon when Jack turned toward home. With all the feverish running around, lately, he had neglected to do his shopping. When he had looked over his stocks in the morning, he had realized that once the can of tomato soup was gone he had nothing else left for his evening meals.

Jack pulled into the crowded parking lot and parked as close as possible to the supermarket.

A half-hour later, he was on his way home once again. The trunk of the car held a few new supplies. He could eat for another week.

At his apartment, he put away the few things that needed refrigerating. He showered before delving into the groceries for dinner ideas. As he stood in the warm downpour, he formulated his plan for the next few days.

An important item on the list was the Saturday evening dinner he and Valerie had planned. The very thought of it brightened his day even more.

But then the realization that he had more to do this evening brought a chill to his thoughts. It was at the same moment that the hot water ran out. *Maybe it's a sign,* he thought.

For a treat, he prepared a frozen chicken dinner and sat in front of the television to watch the news. The usual round of unhappiness was still going on in the world. The weather was due to improve, with the arrival of a 'high' overnight. His favorite hockey team had lost last night's game, but had a chance to pull something off tonight, as long as the injured winger from the opposing team stayed off the ice.

He clicked off the TV and picked up the phone.

Valerie answered after the first ring. They talked about their respective days and where they had been.

After her highway patrol duty, Valerie had had to respond with another officer to a domestic dispute. The husband had been taken into custody for hitting not only his wife but the kids as well. She sounded on the verge of tears as she related her story. Jack offered what little comfort he could.

He told her about the girl outside town, and about the discussions he had had at the police station, both in the morning and afternoon, and about the revelations he had received.

"I've discovered some new evidence. I've pieced together a theory about what happened that night," he said. "I'm not happy with what I'm learning, and I know that when it all comes down there are going to be some pretty devastated people.

"I promise that I won't bring any of this up during our time together tomorrow," he added.

"You'd better not," Val replied. "I'd hate to end up in jail for assault and battery."

Jack could hear her smile in the words.

"I hope to settle a few things in my mind tonight. I have to go out a little later," Jack said. "I'll be around to pick you up just before six tomorrow. The place is busy on the weekend so I had to make reservations. We have a table for six-thirty but I'd like to be there a little earlier."

"Hey, that's fine with me," Val replied. "Show up around noon if you want. I've got nothing else planned."

At the back of his mind, Jack was feeling a desperate need for some sleep. He couldn't be sure when he might wake up and didn't want to disappoint Val by not showing up when he said he would.

They wished each other a good night and hung up. Jack leaned back on the couch and wondered, one more time, whether there was any sort of future with the young policewoman.

"Well, gotta go," he said out loud, and struggled to his feet. "There's work to be done—still." He didn't sound particularly energetic.

Jack dressed for the trip back to town and hurried down to his car.

He knew it was a gamble, but he felt that his best chance to get a clue—even the smallest hint of evidence—would be to go to the one place where most of Rhonda's acquaintances, and Fukushima family friends, could be found. He hoped someone would be in the mood to talk.

As he pulled into the large parking lot behind the ornate white building, the number of vehicles gave him hope. There was always the slim chance that he might get closer to the solution to the puzzle that had so occupied his mind for the past number of days.

Billy Sables knew Jack from their high school days together. His father, Lester, had been the founder of the prominent mortuary. Billy became the owner and head funeral director when Les had retired five years ago. Jack and Billy had met on many occasions since high school. Their chosen professions had brought them together on many a dark day, when crime or an accident reunited them over a dead body. Tonight would be no different.

It was Billy who escorted Jack into the family room, where the Fukushimas were being consoled by their friends and by those who Rhonda had known. The funeral director left his friend to fend for himself and moved down the hall to his office where, he said, another grieving family had plans to make.

Jack noticed that Jimmie Heddon was conspicuously absent. The boy who was, supposedly, so in love with the dead girl, had apparently not bothered to come to the funeral home on the only evening when all her friends would be together.

Nondice Cripps stood by the casket, tears running down her round cheeks, rocking back and forth and quietly humming "Amazing Grace." From time to time she would look at the carefully camouflaged face of her dead friend, and would be gripped with renewed spasms of grief.

Jack was impressed at how well Billy, and his embalmers, had managed to remove the ravages of death and the toll that her sojourn in Dr. Walle's morgue had taken on her flesh.

It was clear that the Fukushimas had their hands full, literally, greeting and receiving condolences from the members of the gathering. In any case, it was not Rhonda's parents Jack had come to see, this time. He waited for the appropriate moment.

"I need your help, again. I'm feeling the pressure of time. Can you point out some of Rhonda's friends to me, and perhaps introduce me? I'd like to ask them a few questions," Jack said, in a hushed voice.

Nondice wiped a tear with her index finger, and nodded to Jack.

"Don Purvis, this here's Mr. Elton," Nondice said, nodding in the investigator's direction. "He's trying to find out who killed Rhonda. He'd like to talk to you."

"Call me Jack." He held out his hand, and received a damp, weak palm from the young man in the ill-fitting tweed jacket.

"Pleased to meet you, I guess," Don replied.

"Let's get out of this crowd for a moment. I think there's an empty room just down the hall," Jack said.

Jack led. When he turned, and entered an empty family room, the young man looked about cautiously, as if expecting there might be another body on display.

"Have a seat," Jack instructed, indicating a couch by the wall. "I'd like to ask you a few questions about Rhonda. Anything you can tell me would be helpful. Is that okay with you?"

"I guess." Don Purvis stared at his hands, then wiped the palms on his pant legs.

"Can you think of anyone who might have wanted to kill Rhonda? As far as you know, was she in any kind of trouble?"

"Well, she was in trouble, you know, like . . . she was expecting a baby. It was a guy named Jimmie Heddon that got her that way."

"I know Jimmie."

"He said he was okay with that, but I don't know. Jimmie and me didn't talk much. I haven't seen him since Rhonda died. Jimmie runs with a different crowd a lot of the time. They are people I don't know. Tougher people. But, no, I can't think of anyone who'd want her dead."

"How about her family?"

"I only know about her parents. I mean, I don't know them personally but, gosh, they really loved her, from what I hear. Her dad was especially protective. Wanted her home at a specific time each night. Checked up on what she was wearing. We kinda got used to arranging our parties and such to fit her schedule.

"There was lots of stuff Ronnie didn't agree with, as far as her parents' expectations were concerned, but one thing she always did was make sure she was home by nine every night. I know it sounds weird but, if she wasn't, her father would get really bent, if you know what I mean. She couldn't even take a job at a burger place that wanted her to do night shifts. We all felt sorry for her."

Not a lot of new information there, Jack thought, as he shook Don Purvis' damp, limp hand, and thanked him.

When he returned to the room where the Fukushimas were greeting, Jack was disappointed to discover that many of the visitors had left. Family members sat around the room, but Nondice and a young, dark-haired girl appeared to be the only friends of Rhonda who remained.

Jen Snyder had met Rhonda when they had worked side-by-side for a week, at the insurance company where Jen was an agent. The two had become fast friends, and had introduced each other to their friends. It had been through Jen that Rhonda had met Jimmie.

"Ronnie and me used to hang together," the Snyder girl said, chewing vigorously on her gum. "I was completely blown away when I heard she'd been offed by persons unknown. I tell you, it makes a person think—about their mortality and all.

"She was such a nice girl. Just like one of us, even though she was, you know, what do they call it, Asian and all."

Jack bit his tongue, and asked, "So, you were surprised by her murder. You never had any indication that someone might want to kill her?"

"No. Not really," Jen said, around a wad of green gum. "Only Jimmie."

"Why Jimmie?"

"Well, Ronnie was pregnant, and it came as a surprise, I gather."

"How so?" Jack asked, waiting for the same answer he had heard from others.

"Well, I think it was miscommunication really." She chewed more vigorously and her eyes rolled up, looking for the right words, Jack supposed. "Jimmie was expecting that Ronnie was taking precautions and I think she was kind of depending on him. But Jimmie told me he suspected she had done this to make him make up his mind to get married."

"There was some doubt about their getting married?" Jack asked.

"Nah. They had pretty much decided, but Ronnie once told me she wanted to get out of her parents' place as soon as she could."

"You think that Jimmie was angry enough to kill her for forcing him into something he wasn't ready for yet?"

"Well, no," Jen said. "But people, you know, say stuff when they are angry that they don't really mean. Jimmie was a little ticked when Ronnie told him she was in a family way."

"And you'd say Rhonda was anxious to leave home?"

"Oh, you bet. She was really under her father's thumb. She loved him, but he really cramped her style, if you get my drift."

Indeed, Jack got the drift. He was feeling snowed under. He walked Jen back to the family room, and reunited her with Nondice Cripps. He followed them out of the building, leaving the Fukushima family to comfort one another as best they could.

Jack drove home, feeling that he had only got a little more information than before. A pattern had emerged, however, that was confirming the suspicions raised by the man he had spoken to, earlier in the day.

In his apartment, again, Jack sat down to try to organize his thoughts, and the notes he had made before he had left the funeral home. When Jack opened his eyes again, almost two hours had passed.

He picked up his notes, and read them over again. He made notes beside the notes. He pondered little things that hadn't seemed important before. Snippets of conversations that he had had with Brendan and his staff came back to him. He noted the important ones.

His mind went to the loving mother and father who wanted the very best for their daughter, but who were not quite ready to let her fully give herself over to western culture. He thought about what a struggle it must be for them, even now, to try to deal with their grief in an atmosphere that did not completely lend itself to their way of handling death.

Rhonda's friends had been devastated by her murder. She had spoken to them with hope for her future. She had intended to make something of herself, and thought she was in line for a permanent job. No more running around from place to place doing a little secretarial work here, office cleaning there, and who knows what else. Instead she ended up dead, on the floor of an office, where she thought her future would begin.

Jimmie Heddon was a rough sort. If she hadn't made him her man of choice, perhaps she wouldn't have been carrying the added burden of pregnancy out of wedlock. But it seemed to Jack that her friends believed that Jimmie intended to make things right, or at least better. They had been planning a wedding, after all. When Jack and Valerie had spoken with the young man, he had shown that he did have a tender side. If he had been treating Rhonda anything like he was his mother, there was every reason to believe the two of them could have made a go of it; could have raised a happy family. On the other hand, Jimmie had shown that he had a volatile anger. What might it take to set him off into a homicidal rage?

Was he right about his suspicions? Could he go ahead and press for a confession? As he thought over the little bit of sleuthing that he had been able to do, he knew that there were times he had misinterpreted things that were said. One vital piece of information had been flip-flopped in his memory, and had slowed things down.

A question hovered in Jack's mind. One person could answer it. If the answer was what he suspected, all the rest would likely fall into place. If he was wrong, he would have to toss out the case he was building, and start again. He would do that too. He was becoming obsessed with the riddle as much as with finding the culprit.

He knew this. One of the people on his list had met with Rhonda on that fateful night, and had deprived her of her life and her future. In the process, her unborn baby had been prevented from experiencing any life at all. Jack allowed himself to wonder if it would be such a wise thing to be born into a world and an environment where there was such violence, and people who held life itself in such low esteem.

Now he was really depressed. He hoped that what he had to do in the next few days would not taint the happiness he had expected to experience during his time with Valerie Cummins.

He realized he would need a clear mind to sort out the information he had about Rhonda, her family, and her friends, limited though that information was. He allowed his thoughts to turn to other things.

Jack washed up the cutlery, from the dinner he had eaten earlier in the evening, and threw out the tin plate on which it had been cooked. It was at times like these that he began to consider, anew, the other benefits of having a wife.

It was lonely living alone. It was boring eating packaged food. Jack had never been much of a cook, and his disasters outweighed his successes in the culinary department. He wondered if Valerie was any good at meal preparation.

Jack marveled at how quickly he had become enamored with the woman. It surprised him, too, that she had so readily accepted his offers of friendship and companionship. He wondered if this was just meant to be, or whether his bubble was going to burst, and she would not want him in her life anymore.

I shouldn't think too deeply about these things. I talk my-self into a depression, worrying about how something good might go bad.

He had no doubt, Valerie was a good thing.

He thought about her for a moment. He meditated fully on his plans for the next evening. He imagined what she might look like, dressed for an evening on the town. He smiled to himself. The cloud was lifting. He determined to hold on to the good thoughts. He was glad that the two had promised to stay away from talking shop. He wondered if he would be able to uphold his end of the bargain.

He turned out the apartment lights and headed to bed, hoping to dream of Valerie, and not the state of the world.

Chapter Twenty-seven

Jack enjoyed the weekends. They were an opportunity to unwind, and gain some fresh perspective. Ordinarily, it meant he could take a rest from chasing after people who hadn't paid their bills, or who were being subpoenaed to give evidence in a minor court case. Sometimes, in this line of work, the reason why a person did not pay up was evident. He had visited enough hovels in his travels to know that some folks got desperate and did desperate things to try to provide for their families.

On the other side were the individuals who were out to scam as many people as they could, and who made it their daily task to take as much as they could, with as little effort as possible. They were good at what they did, and sometimes got away with it. Jack never got to see what happened after he had passed the papers along. He never knew whether these folks received their just rewards. He sometimes wished that the less fortunate ones, the desperate ones, might be cut a little slack. It wasn't fair to bend the law, but sometimes it seemed to Jack that it might be more compassionate.

He thought about the times when it was not the adults, but their children, who suffered. He could still remember the time he was called upon to reclaim a kid's bicycle.

The boy had a birthday coming up, and desperately wanted a bike. The kid was a good-hearted sort, and had taken on a paper route to try to make a little money for himself so his parents wouldn't have to pay him an allowance.

His father thought a two-wheeler would help, but he had no ready cash. He had bought the thing on credit, and presented it to his son. The young fellow had been overjoyed with the gift, and used it on his new paper route.

Unfortunately, the money that dad had been expecting from a part-time job didn't materialize, and Jack was called to handle the repossession. He went to the house and comforted the father, who was, needless to say, devastated by the unhappy turn of events.

The boy had arrived home as Jack was taking the bicycle away. The dad had a difficult time explaining things to his son, who was beside himself with grief. Not only had he lost his bike, he had lost faith in his father.

Jack wondered if things were ever put right again.

This weekend was so different, in many ways. Jack hadn't been serving papers lately. His recent sleuthing activities had probably shortened the odds on his returning to that line of work or, if he did, profiting from it. It was likely that he had lost some of his clients since spending so much of his time with the Rhonda Fukushima case, but he wanted to finish what he had started. He wanted to be there when the arrest was made.

Jack had awakened mid-morning and taken his time getting out of bed. He was happy, knowing that he did not have to rush out anywhere, and that his day could be work-free, if he so chose. He could hear the traffic passing by, under his window.

Saturday was a busy day downtown, but for different reasons than during the week. It was a day for shopping. School was out, so there would be roaming bands of teenagers, visiting with their friends, spending allowances, and trying to make those connections, and establish the relationships, that their young hormones dictated were mandatory. In the afternoon, the local theaters would be almost full. The matinée crowd took advantage of the reduced prices; not the ten and twenty-five cents of years gone by, but at least a two dollar discount from the eight or ten dollar admission that would be charged at night. Allowances had gone up to match inflation. Jack thought about the kid, and the bike, again.

The Fukushima family came to mind. This afternoon they would lay their daughter to rest. The Les Sables Funeral Home would, no doubt, do its very best to help them in their time of grief. Jack wondered what sort of service they would have. With such a large Japanese population, the funeral home was likely well-practiced in dealing with traditional services. Jack didn't even know where someone would go to find whatever clergy were necessary for such a thing. He was unaware of what religion the Fukushimas might be. He wasn't convinced that any religion would have the resources to provide the comfort that the Fukushimas would need in the face of such a tragedy.

"Enough of this lying around," Jack said, out loud, as he snapped the covers off, and felt the cold air of the room. "I've got a date with a beautiful girl tonight. Gotta get ready."

He grabbed a bathrobe, and headed for the shower. As the warm water washed over him, he hummed to himself, trying to concentrate on the evening's plans, and to keep the murder out of his mind.

Jack dressed casually for the afternoon. He considered Valerie's suggestion that they spend the afternoon together, and wondered if the invitation still stood. He decided he would check it out, after he had some food in his stomach.

While he could bypass breakfast on other days, on Saturday and Sunday Jack would wake up hungry. He could not function on those two days without a hearty brunch.

Today was scrambled eggs with ham, and a side of toast and jam. These were things he could prepare without destroying the food. The eggs were scrambled because he had learned, early on, that he was all thumbs when it came to breaking eggs. If his plan was to break the yolks intentionally he could be sure of success in that. He just had to remember to keep the eggs from burning. He had developed a process that seemed to work. He would heat the pan and add the eggs. He would stir up the mixture until things started to congeal. By taking the pan off the stove, the eggs would usually finish cooking, by themselves, without the aid of the stove element.

He had bought his ham pre-sliced and pre-cooked. This he would throw into the pan, after he had removed the eggs, and place it over the element, which he would allow to heat again and immediately turn off. In theory, by the time the toast was ready, the ham would be warmed through, and all would be well. Sometimes, though, he forgot to turn down the element. On those mornings, he had scrambled eggs, toast, and dark brown meat that tasted like leather and looked like a hockey puck.

Today he was focused, and the meal came together just as he had planned it. He made some coffee, and sat at his little kitchen table while he ate.

Just after the noon hour, Jack decided to see if Valerie's schedule for the afternoon was still open. While he had promised they would not talk about work during dinner, he had made no such vow with regard to other times. And he had a few things he wanted to run by her, to see what she thought. He hoped she could tell him if he was on the right track.

The phone rang twice before the receiver was picked up. He loved the sound of her voice, and she had said hello twice before he caught his breath enough to respond.

"I knew it was you," she said.

"How did you know it was me?"

"You're the only one who ever calls." She giggled.

"Okay Carnak, what am I calling about?"

"Hey, only one mind-reading trick per customer. You tell me why you called. I'll let you know if you're right." She giggled, again.

"Very funny. I was wondering if you had a few moments to spare this afternoon. I'll warn you, I want to talk business. Got some ideas that need a clear thinker."

"You can't get your mind off that case for a moment, can you?"

"If what I have in mind is correct, I won't have to think about it for much longer. Do you want to help me deal with my addiction?"

"Sure. Why not? But you need to know I've got a hot date tonight. You'll have to leave so I can get ready."

"You've got a date too? Isn't that a coincidence? So do I."

They bantered back and forth a little more before deciding that Jack would drive around to Valerie's apartment as soon as he had dressed.

He chose the best looking of his casual wardrobe for the encounter, and headed downstairs. He made a detour to the office on the second floor, first. He gathered up the small pile of mail behind the door, and reset his answering machine. The messages held no interest for the process server turned private eye.

On his trip across town, Jack passed the street that led to Chinatown, and the enclave where many Asian cultures came together. He thought, again, of the Fukushimas, and what they were doing this afternoon. He felt sorry for them, and not just because of what this day would require of them.

The curb, on the street where Valerie lived, was lined with cars. Jack had to go a couple of blocks further to find a parking spot. He regretted that the walk back took precious moments from the time he would have preferred to spend with his friend, who was also becoming a sidekick of sorts. *Holmes and Watson*, he thought, but only briefly. Watson just couldn't compare to Val. *Not as smart, either*, he reflected further.

The lobby of the building was typical. A row of buttons ran down the side of a glassed-in list of the tenants. A locked door separated the entryway from the rest of the building.

Jack scanned the list until he found 'Cummins, VL.' He poked the button beside the listing.

"Yes, who is it?" a disembodied female voice asked.

"Cable guy."

"How do I know it's really you?"

"You stopped me for driving the other day. How's that?"

"Okay, you can pass. But it wasn't driving. It was speeding."

The door buzzed. Jack pulled it open and stepped through.

The buzzer continued for a while longer, then fell silent. Val's apartment number, by the entryway, was listed as two-zero-seven. Jack assumed that she lived on the second floor. A sign indicated that there was an elevator in the corridor. He followed the arrow, and then watched the numbers change as he was taken up one floor in the small, hydraulic lift.

Valerie's apartment was on the back side of the building. All the odd numbers ran along that side. He rapped gently on number two-zero-seven.

She greeted him, wearing jeans and a T-shirt. Her hair was in a ponytail. Jack noticed she had bare feet.

She led him down a short hallway to a living room containing a couch and an easy chair, both upholstered in cream-colored fabric. The walls were off-white, and a beige carpet covered the floor. A small kitchen was visible through a door to one side.

The walls were adorned with various prints. On one side was a series of certificates Valerie had received at the police academy. They indicated various courses she had been successful in completing. One was a citation for excellence in marksmanship. Her graduation certificate was in the center of the display, bearing the bison head crest of the RCMP.

Valerie offered coffee or a cold drink. Jack settled for water, with a twist of lemon. She poured herself a cola, and curled up on the easy chair. Jack chose the end of the couch furthest from her. No use seeming too forward, too soon, he figured. This was business, for now, after all. He did not feel quite the same uneasiness, today, that he had felt the day before when he had been alone with Nondice Cripps.

"You had some things you wanted to discuss about the

Fukushima case," Val said. "I gather, from the way you sounded on the phone, you have been thinking about this all night."

"You could tell?"

"I could tell. I hope you will be a little more jovial on our date tonight."

"Help me now, and I can guarantee it, I think."

Valerie set down her glass and gave her attention entirely to the man at the other end of the couch. She leaned her chin on the palm of her right hand and looked at him with intense blue eyes.

"I'm listening," she said.

Jack reviewed the results of his interviews, and the security video that had confirmed his friend's alibi. Valerie knew, first-hand, about the talk with Jimmie Heddon.

"I'm still a little uncomfortable with his attitude, Jack. Jimmie could bear some watching. Is he one of your suspects, still?"

"I've got a few more questions to ask him, before I make any final deductions."

Valerie listened attentively, as he shared more of the details he had gleaned from Rhonda's friends, and the message she had received, inviting her to the offices of Biggs, Wilberforce, Hutton, and Small, for an interview.

"From what you've told me about Mr. and Mrs. Fukushima, they have an interesting history. I can't say that I agree with all of their beliefs, but there's no denying they loved their daughter. Have you spoken to them again, lately?"

"I intend to pay them another visit once they have had the opportunity to honor their late daughter properly. Buddhists, if that's what they are, consider death a beginning, and usually think of the funeral ceremony as a celebration. But, I'm afraid that the circumstances surrounding Rhonda's death have made that all but impossible. I'll let them have some time together, before I talk to them again about my investigation."

Over the next hour or so, Jack laid out for Valerie his theories about what had happened and why.

"So what do you think?" he asked when he was done.

"It sounds like a sad scenario. If what you say is true, it sounds like a logical explanation."

"What do you think I should do?"

"I agree," Val replied. "You need to do some more talking, before you start making accusations. I'd run your thoughts past Brown and Willis if your conclusion is the same after the interviews. If they agree, and only if they agree, they will take it from there."

"Do you think they'll think I'm crazy?"

"Probably. But tell them what your friend said. He's an authority on these things from the sound of it. They can check it out with him too."

Jack smiled across the space between them.

"Okay, that's it. No more business today. I'm switching to 'date mode' from here on in. Gotta be in the right frame of mind for dinner. Work gives me indigestion," he said.

Valerie looked at her watch.

"All right, session's over," she said. "I have to get ready for a night on the town. You can't be here when my date shows up."

"That will be tricky." Jack smiled.

"I'm expecting a guy in a suit and tie."

"That, I can arrange. See you in an hour and a half."

She showed him to the door. He thanked her for her help. He took another ride on the elevator.

The afternoon traffic was a little more dense than before, as people headed home. Soon there would be a heavier flow back into town to enjoy the nightlife. Jack would be among that group. He resolved not to let anything get in the way of his enjoying the evening with Valerie.

Chapter Twenty-eight

Jack took special care preparing for the evening out. He showered for the second time that day. This time he shaved with a blade rather than his old Remington to make sure that his face was smooth. One never knew when it might be advantageous to be kissable, he told himself.

He had one laundered shirt that he kept for occasions such as this, and his best suit was the only thing that would do for a night on the town with a beautiful woman. He splashed on a little cologne to complete his ensemble.

The ninety minutes had passed quickly while Jack was preening and fussing over his appearance for Valerie's benefit. Once again, he was standing in the lobby of her apartment building, pressing the button beside number 207.

Valerie buzzed him in. A woman transformed opened the door. The jeans and T had been exchanged for a pink dress that displayed her attributes to advantage. She wore high-heeled shoes. Her hair was down and, in the interim between their afternoon parting and their reunion, she had curled it. If Jack had not fully appreciated her beauty before, his mind more than compensated for it now. He considered himself a very fortunate man as he stood, with his mouth open, and nothing to say.

"Ready to go?" she asked.

"Uh, yeah. Wow, you are something to behold."

"Why thank you sir. I appreciate it. You are a fine looking gentleman yourself, if I do say so."

"No, I'm serious. You're beautiful."

"I'm serious too," she replied.

She took his arm.

Jack had managed to find a parking spot close to the front of the apartment building. He held the door for Valerie to get in this time, before going around to the driver's side.

"This certainly is shaping up to be a beautiful evening," Jack said, as they drove along the ocean shoreline toward the restaurant.

"This is a lovely city. There is so much to see. We don't have anything like this where I come from," Val said. "Some places, on the prairies, there is no water anywhere in sight and, where there is anything significant you can still see the other shore. Apart from that, there is nothing but miles and miles of miles and miles."

"I've been to Alberta and Saskatchewan," Jack said. "I know exactly what you're talking about. Of course, I can't say I've lived there like you can. Every part of the country has its own special attraction. Some folks can't live in the mountains because they feel boxed in."

"Oh, I love the mountains. I'd love to have a little cabin someplace, where I could get away from the busyness of the city," Val said.

"But you like the city, too, you just said."

"Love it here. It's just that it would be nice to get away once in awhile."

"I feel that way sometimes too," Jack said.

When they arrived at the restaurant, the place was crowded. Jack was glad he had made the effort to ask for a reservation. Jack and Valerie were taken directly to a table that looked out toward the water and the setting sun.

The greeter handed them menus, and informed them that their server would be with them shortly. They studied the large folders, as if preparing for an exam. Neither spoke, as they considered the long list of possibilities. When they had decided what they would ask for, they looked out over the picturesque scene that was unfolding to the west. Both agreed it was much better than watching TV at home. Alone.

Jack ordered wine to go with the meal and placed orders for them both. With the sun finally below the horizon, the lights of the boats in the harbor twinkled on, and the city lights reflected off the water.

Valerie had a look of contentment. Jack knew that he was happier than he had been in a long time. For tonight, the concerns of the past little while, and the challenges that would face him next week, were forgotten.

They looked into each other's eyes and a communication passed between them, that this would be a special night to be savored. Jack reached across the table to take Valerie's hand. At that moment, their waiter arrived with a huge tray bearing their meal. Jack withdrew his hand. Valerie watched it go. They would eat first.

They spoke little during the meal. Jack's steak was cooked to perfection and, although he had never been a particular fan of vegetables, he had to admit that even that part of the dinner was very tasty. Valerie had chosen a seafood platter, and informed Jack that it was the best she had had in a long time.

Soon the plates were cleared away, and the coffee was brought. The two of them seemed at a loss for words. They basked in the warmth of the moment. Again, Jack reached across the table. This time he managed to take hold of Valerie's hand. She looked from their joined hands, deep into his eyes.

"Thank you," she said.

"You're welcome."

"I mean it. This has been—still is—a wonderful night. You have made me feel special, and I appreciate that."

Jack did not know what to say, so he just kept looking at her—and held on. He noticed that she had tears in her eyes.

"Is something wrong?" he asked.

"Not at all. I'm just so happy. I'm just glad to be here with you."

Jack was struck dumb again. No woman had ever said that to him before.

"Do we want dessert?" he asked, finally.

"I couldn't eat another thing. Can we go for a walk?" She indicated an illuminated walkway that skirted the harbor.

Jack paid the bill, and added a substantial tip. They left the restaurant and walked in the moonlight, neither one saying anything.

The night air was getting cooler. The dampness from the water added to the chill. Valerie drew closer to Jack. He put his arm around her to offer a little extra warmth. Eventually, they reached the end of the walkway, and had to start the walk back. The last lamppost was dark. Valerie turned toward Jack and looked up at him.

"I have had a wonderful time. I want to thank you," she said.

She put her arm around his neck so he had to bring his face close to hers. They stood together in a warm embrace. She kissed him. It was a while before they began the journey back to the car.

"Let's go back to my place," she said.

Jack was in too good a mood to even consider refusing.

They walked arm-in-arm back to the car. Jack removed his jacket, and placed it around Valerie's shoulders to help keep the chill away. They drove without saying a word but there was music playing in Jack's heart. He looked over at his passenger. Contentment was still evident on her face.

After parking, the two walked hand-in-hand into Valerie's building. She let them both in, and they rode the elevator to the second floor.

"Just have a seat in the living room, and I'll put on a pot of coffee," she said as she unlocked her door.

"I'll try to be patient." Jack gave her hand a squeeze, and let her go.

Valerie puttered around in the kitchen, putting water in the coffee maker, and hunting in the fridge. Jack got an occasional glimpse of her, as she moved back and forth past the kitchen door.

While the coffee was brewing, Valerie came back to be with Jack but, unlike their afternoon encounter, she did not take the easy chair. Instead, she sat close beside him on the couch.

"I'm so glad we could go out together tonight. You're such a special person to me. I feel safe when I'm with you," she said.

She moved closer, and leaned over to put her head on his shoulder.

"And here I thought I was the one who should feel safe, having my very own police officer as an escort," Jack said.

He put his arm around her, and held her close.

"Remember what we said before. I'm not a cop tonight, and you're not investigating anything. We're just two people, together, enjoying each other's company."

She lifted her head, looked at him intently, and smiled that smile that melted his heart.

"I'm afraid," Jack said. The tone of his voice startled Valerie.

"What's wrong, Jack?"

"I'm just afraid midnight is going to come, and one of us is going to turn into a pumpkin."

"Silly."

"Tonight has been special for me too," Jack said. "I can't remember when I've enjoyed a more satisfying evening. I'm afraid it might turn out to be too good to be true."

"Well, you have nothing to fear from my end. Relax. Believe in yourself. Believe in me."

They sat for a long while without speaking; just enjoying the warmth of each other's touch. Eventually, Valerie gathered herself enough to go to the kitchen and pour their coffee. With it, she brought out two of the largest slices of cheesecake Jack had ever seen.

"It's a celebration," she said. "I made it my self."

"No fooling?"

"Yes, fooling. But I bought it myself. That should count for something, don't you think?"

"You are very thoughtful."

"Thanks."

Jack stayed a while longer. They talked and ate. The conversation centered on getting to know one another. Jack shared a little of his background, growing up in Quebec. He shared how he had ended up leaving police work and taking on other jobs.

Valerie talked about her family on the prairies, and how tough her mother was finding 'her little girl' living so far away from home and working in a job that held so much potential danger.

"If she knew you were with me tonight, she would really worry about you," Jack said.

"She knows about us. She hopes to get to meet you sometime. Soon."

Jack rolled his eyes and leaned back on the couch. Valerie leaned over and kissed his cheek.

"Am I moving too fast?" she asked.

Jack helped Valerie clean away the dishes. It was past midnight as they stood by the door of the apartment, in a warm embrace.

"I'll call you tomorrow—um, today, but later," he said.

"After noon would be best. Sunday is my day to get up late, and move slow, if you know what I mean." Val smiled as she opened the apartment door.

"I can see where we're going to continue to get along just fine."

He kissed her, and held her tightly. He really hated to have to tear himself away. They waved to each other, when he turned back toward her, halfway down the hall.

Jack was suddenly in front of his building. It seemed as if he had traveled home in a bubble. That bubble would break and he would have to return to the challenges that faced him with the dawn of the next day. For now, there would be the rest of this Sunday to relax, regroup, and reflect. He went to bed reflecting on the love that had come into his life.

* * *

The ringing of the phone awakened him from a deep slumber. The numerals on the clock radio informed him that it was almost noon. He hadn't even begun his brunch ritual yet.

"Hello, Jack here."

"Hi Jack. Guess who?"

Valerie sounded in one of her playful moods. It took Jack a little longer to get up to speed.

"Hi, sweetie. What can I do for you today?" he asked.

"I was getting lonely and just wondering how you were."

"Not bad. I had a wonderful time last night. I hope you feel the same way."

"I told you so last night."

"Just as long as you feel the same way this morning—er, afternoon—whatever it is right now."

Jack yearned to see Valerie again, but knew that the preparation for what he would have to do in the next couple of days would be on his mind. He did not broach the subject.

An hour later, they were approaching the end of their conversation. Jack suggested another night out. Valerie accepted.

"Let me know how everything goes. Okay?" she said.

"I'll give you a call, in the evening, tomorrow. Maybe we can do coffee together, so I can debrief."

"Sounds good to me. I should be finished work around three. I'm free after that."

"I'll call. Bye for now."

"Bye. I'll be waiting. Love ya!"

Only after he hung up did Valerie's parting comment register in his mind. He was happy. He realized he loved her too. He wished he had told her so. He dialed her number.

The rest of the afternoon went by quickly. Jack had felt only a little foolish calling Valerie back. He was glad that he had and, by the sound of her voice, she had been more than pleased to hear that he had the same sort of feelings for her. They agreed to take it slowly.

Jack reviewed his paperwork one more time to be sure that he had everything in order. He came away convinced that he had missed something but there didn't seem to be anything out of place. The next day's encounters would tell the final tale.

Chapter Twenty-nine

When Jack entered Fukushima's he did not immediately see the little man. The store was empty that early in the morning. Tourists were either out and about, visiting points of interest, or had not risen from slumber, due to exhaustion from the previous day's activities, or an evening of late-night revelry.

As he moved toward the back of the shop, where Mr. Fukushima had his table and chairs set for tea, Jack heard a sound like a pop, followed by a ripping noise. It was coming from another room at the very rear. The door stood ajar. The sound was repeated.

When Jack knocked on the door, he heard a sharp intake of breath followed by a grunt, and the sound of shuffling feet.

The door opened the rest of the way, and Jack could see that this was a storeroom. Boxes were piled along the walls, from ceiling to floor. Most bore printing that indicated that their origin was Asia. Two of the cartons sat in the middle of the floor with their flaps open and bubble wrap sticking through the top.

Mr. Fukushima held a folding pocket knife, point to the ceiling, in front of his face. When he saw Jack, he gave a little bow of welcome, folded the implement, and stuck it in a sheath on his belt.

It was then that it dawned on Jack that the sound he had heard, as he approached, was the knife piercing the packing tape, followed by the old man slicing between the flaps of the boxes.

"That's a nice knife you have there," Jack said.

"I always carry a knife," Fukushima responded, patting the leather holster housing his makeshift box cutter.

"Some reason for that?"

"When I was young, I met up with some bad men. They hurt me badly." The memory caused pain to cross the old man's face. "I decided to protect myself."

"But you can't carry something like that on the street," Jack said.

"I only use it in my shop, now. Open boxes. No more bad men, but handy if someone wants to try to rob Fukushima, you know. I keep it in the case when I'm on the street."

"I see your point." Jack really did see the point. The man was not a particularly menacing individual, and there were, unfortunately, some people who might want to rob him. If he greeted them with the blade, as he had just welcomed Jack, they might have second thoughts. Jack wondered, though, how quickly those old hands could get the knife open.

"Would you like some tea?" the shopkeeper asked. "My wife told me you were here last week, while I was . . ." His voice trailed off, and he shuffled past Jack to his little oasis at the back of the shop. There, he plugged in a small kettle, then set about arranging cups, and measuring green tea into a small pot. "Please. Sit," he said.

"Thank you, sir. I just have a few questions to ask you, and then I'll be on my way."

Mr. Fukushima looked troubled as he took a seat, across from Jack.

"It has been a troublesome week for us. We buried our daughter on Saturday. My wife is preparing to fly back to Japan this week, to take our Ronnie's ashes to be buried with other family members." He shook his head, and stared at the floor.

"Again, my sympathies to you and your family. I have been trying to bring this to a conclusion for you. I have been speaking to Rhonda's friends to see if they can help. I visited with Mr. Heddon, as well."

"He's responsible for my daughter dying," Fukushima said, with another sad shake of the head.

"You said that when I spoke to you before. Do you really think James was your daughter's killer?"

"He is responsible." The man's voice had a note of finality about it.

"The police are continuing their investigation, of course, but are not hopeful that they have the resources to arrest someone any time soon. If there is not a break in the case . . ."

"Break? What does this mean? 'Break in the case.' I do not understand."

"If the police cannot determine who killed someone within the first forty-eight hours, it is highly unlikely that they will come up with a quick solution. In Rhonda's case, it has been almost two weeks. The police must concentrate on a number of different things. After a while, they have to move on and hope that some new evidence comes to light.

"I'm still involved because a friend of mine has been suspected of being your daughter's killer. His name is Brendan Biggs. He works up the street, at the advertising agency Biggs, Wilberforce, Hutton, and Small. The reason he is under suspicion is because your daughter had a note saying she was to meet Mr. Biggs the night she died."

"Mr. Biggs did not kill my Ronnie. You can tell the police."

"I'm glad to hear you say that, sir. You've told me that you think James Heddon is responsible. I just wish it was that easy to convince them. If only she hadn't had that note."

"I'm very sorry," the older man said. He rose to unplug the kettle. "We must wait for the water, now. Green tea must not be made with boiling water. We wait a few minutes."

"Did you take the phone call about the job she was being offered at Mr. Biggs' company?"

The man hesitated before answering. "I gave Ronnie the note."

"It was okay with you that she went out to the office building that night?"

"The water is ready. Excuse me, please." Fukushima rose and went about the task of steeping the tea leaves. When he was done, he returned with the pot, and took his seat again.

"I can see that you are quite distressed by what I have been telling you," Jack said. "I won't bother you with any more questions, for now. Let's have our tea."

Jack's host gave a nod, and began filling the cups.

As the two men sat together, at the back of the souvenir shop, the old man spoke of his life in another country, and the traditions of his ancestors.

"I should have known—should have understood—that my Ronnie would want to fit in with this culture. But we had not brought her up that way. She did not want to follow our old ways."

"I understand that that was a concern to you, sir," Jack said.

"Yes, that is true. A great deal of trouble has come from her failure to honor our traditions."

Jack soon finished his tea and thanked his host.

"I wonder if you might like to come with me, later today, to see the place where your daughter died. It might help you to deal with what has happened to Rhonda. I don't know much about your religion, but it might give you an opportunity to alleviate your sorrow."

In Jack's mind were visions of the makeshift shrines that sprung up along roads and highways when young people lost their lives in auto accidents. Some years ago a young girl had been murdered under a bridge not far from town. For weeks, people came to that spot and left flowers or slowed their vehicles in honor of the life that had been lost.

He wasn't expecting a shrine to rise on the office desks. He envisioned another way that Rhonda Fukushima could find rest for her soul.

"That would be helpful," the older man said. He rose from his chair and walked, with Jack, to the front door, before bidding him good-bye.

Out on the sidewalk, Jack turned and watched as Mr. Fukushima returned to his unopened boxes. Then he walked over to the sandwich board that directed visitors to the front door of the souvenir shop. He looked at it for a long time.

Jack needed to talk to Jimmie Heddon. He wanted to have his conversation out of earshot of the young man's mother. He still didn't know where Heddon worked, so would have to deal with mom first. He went in search of a pay phone.

Jack did not introduce himself on the phone, except to say he needed to get in touch with Jimmie, right away. The man's mother did not bother to challenge him but simply explained that her son worked at a warehouse on the edge of town. Jack wrote the address on the back of an old envelope he found in his jacket pocket.

He found the warehouse where Jimmie Heddon worked in a run-down section of the city. Older buildings had been converted, and re-converted to suit various proprietors over the years. The building was a low-lying monster, crouched on the back of a lot whose paving had seen years of hard use. He drove to the office door, weaving between upraised chunks of asphalt and water-filled potholes. He was glad that he hadn't succumbed to the temptation to buy a new car.

"Jim's out on a delivery right now. He'll be back in time for lunch. He never misses lunch. I'd invite you to wait in here but, as you can see, we don't have a lot of space for visitors."

This welcome was coming from an unshaven, flannel-shirted office manager with a dead cigarette hanging from his lips. He walked about as he spoke, stuffing folders into a rack on the wall. The file holders bore the names of the various warehouse workers. Jack recognized the name Jim Heddon, taped to the front of one of the cubbyholes.

He checked his watch. He would wait in the car. He thanked the man behind the office counter.

Jack appreciated predictable people. It made his job a little easier to bear, when folks did what others predicted they would do.

Jimmie Heddon pulled into the lot in one of the warehouse trucks just before noon. Jack noticed the printed paper bag, with a bright red, stylized M printed on it, which the young man carried into the office.

He gave Jimmie a moment or two to do his paperwork and then went in. Jack hoped that he would not meet with the same reaction he had witnessed the last time the two of them had stood face-to-face. He was ready if it came to blows.

"Oh, it's you again." The tone was more frustration than anger. Jack was relieved.

"Hi, Jimmie. I really need to talk to you. I've got a few questions that need answering. Now, you don't have to talk to me, if you don't want to, but it's better here than downtown."

Jack left it at that. He had no authority to take the young man into custody. If pressed, he would have to say that, if Jimmie didn't talk here, they would have to meet downtown somewhere. Certainly not at the police station. He was depending on his interviewee not to press for further clarification.

"Okay. I've certainly got nothing to hide. We've got a lunchroom. It's not much but at least we can sit down."

Jack followed Jimmie to a grimy room off the office. Chairs that had seen better days flanked a couple of round metal tables.

"It's a little dirty in here but it's clean dirt. Just can't keep the place spotless when you're handling all sorts of stuff all day long. Grease and dirt gets on your clothes, and rubs off on the seats, and anything else you touch. Just remember to wash your hands when you leave."

With that, the young man reached into the pocket of his pants and pulled out a folding knife. He opened it, and began cleaning under his nails with the point of the blade. When he was done he wiped it on a pant-leg, folded it, and stuffed it back in his pocket.

"That's what my mom always says," he continued. "Wash your hands and wear clean underwear. If I ever get hit by a truck, I'm all set. Now, what sort of things did you want to know?"

Jack took a deep breath. This was going to lead back to the topic of conversation that got him expelled from the Heddon residence only a few days ago.

"Jimmie, I really need to ask if you know anything about Rhonda's death. Where were you that night?"

"Look. I'm sorry about the other night," the young man offered.

Jack felt his chest loosen a little. He breathed easier now.

"I knew my mom was listening, and I needed to get you to leave. I knew that if you really wanted some information it wouldn't be long before you'd track me down. I feel a little more comfortable talking about this here."

"Where were you on the night of Rhonda's death?"

"I was here. I needed some extra cash for a trip I was planning—for my honeymoon—with Rhonda."

"You're telling me you were working, and that you were planning on getting married."

"That's what I'm saying. And that was part of why I got a little hot under the collar the other night. Why would I kill someone I loved; someone who was going to be my wife?"

"Jimmie, we know that Rhonda was pregnant. Was the baby yours?"

"My momma would kill me if she thought I was, you know, doing that, with a woman I wasn't married to—yet. She's kind of old school and all." He looked as if he hoped Jack would understand.

"Was the baby yours?" Jack asked in a more hushed tone. He wasn't sure Jimmie would have wanted to share any of this with his co-workers.

"Yes, it was mine. Ronnie and I had decided that we were going to keep it, and I was planning to marry her. When her old man found out, he was fit to be tied."

"I would be, too, if it was my daughter. Of course I don't have a daughter, or a wife—yet. So this news wasn't too much of a surprise, or a cause of anger, for you?"

"No. Not at all. Well, not after the first shock of realization. I mean, we knew what we were doing, and what we were risking. I guess it wasn't totally unexpected. To be honest, it came at a bad time for both of us. But, you're not suggesting I'd kill a girl over something like that, are you?"

"Others have Jimmie. You wouldn't have been the first. Or the last."

"Only a sicko would do something like that. I don't work that way," the young man said, with apparent conviction.

"So you didn't feel that Rhonda was pressuring you to get married? You didn't think she might have allowed this to happen, in order to force you into it?"

"Do you really think that I'm that crazy that I'd kill Rhonda if I thought she'd done something like that? I might have wondered whether she was wanting me to finally make up my mind. But, I'd never get that angry."

"Mr. Fukushima thinks you've got a pretty bad temper."

"Well, he oughta know. He's set me off enough times with his rants about tradition, and honor, and all that stuff."

Clearly, this was not the time to offer a lecture on Oriental traditions and customs. Not that Jack knew that much about it anyway. He'd just heard the passion in Gregory Fukushima's voice when they had talked about Rhonda.

"He seems to hold you responsible for his daughter's death."

"It doesn't surprise me. The old fool never thought I was

good enough for Ronnie. He hated that she wasn't dating someone with a Japanese background. I might understand if you were trying to find out if I killed *him*. There were times I almost wanted to."

"Almost wanted to?"

"Come on, man, killing is just plain wrong. I thought you'd know that. I just get real angry sometimes."

Yeah, I sort of got that impression, Jack thought.

The young man's eyes started to tear up, and his lower lip trembled. He covered his mouth with his hand, and stared at the grimy tabletop.

Blinking away the tears, Jimmie added, "That's why I didn't go to the funeral parlor to see Rhonda. I was afraid I might have to put up with an attack from her father. I didn't want that. I didn't get to the funeral for the same reason. It was that bad. I never really got to say good-bye."

"I appreciate your being so open about this, Jimmie. You've been a help. You really have." Jack pushed his metal chair back from the table and stood up. "I'll be in touch."

"Let me know if there's anything else I can do to help," Jimmie said, and blew his nose on a hankie he had produced from the back pocket of his grimy work pants. "Just, please, be careful what you say, if you're around my mom. Since dad left us, about four years ago, she's been pretty protective of me, and I guess I've got protective of her. I'd hate for any of this stuff, about my being responsible for the baby, and all, to be a disappointment to her."

"We'll do our best, Jimmie."

Jack inquired about the location of the nearest sink, washed his hands well, and was soon on his way back home, with a head full of new details and a plan for the next day.

He was certain he had found Rhonda's killer. He wasn't at all happy about what he would be called upon to do.

Jack drove to Brendan's office, and made arrangements to come in, later in the evening, with Mr. Fukushima. The ad executive was interested in hearing about the progress Jack had made in the investigation.

"I'm still under suspicion, you know. Apparently another girl was killed a few nights ago. The police were in the office the next morning, asking where I had been the night before. I thought I was in for it again. Fortunately, they caught the guy a few hours later, and I was off the hook. I'll be glad to have some closure for this whole thing."

"I've told Mr. Fukushima that I'm offering him closure to all his concerns, by bringing him up here. I hope it works," Jack said.

"Sure, that will be fine. I'll let the security people know that you are to be given access to the office tonight."

"Thanks. I appreciate that. I hope I can give you some news later this week."

The two men said their farewells. Jack rode the elevator to the lobby. It was too early for Graham, the night watchman, to be on duty.

Jack found a pay phone. He dialed the number he had written on a scrap of paper some days before. He was relieved when the person he most needed to speak to, answered his call.

After concluding his conversation, Jack walked around the corner, to Fukushima's, and told Rhonda's father that he would come by at closing time to escort him up to the offices of Biggs, Wilberforce, Hutton, and Small. The little man looked sad as he accepted the invitation to visit the place where his daughter had spent her final moments. The shop was busy with tourists, so Jack had a good excuse to be on his way with no further conversation.

He drove to police headquarters and made an appointment to meet, the next morning, with Brown and Willis. He returned home, earlier than usual, reminding himself that he would be out later that evening.

Chapter Thirty

The only consolation Jack had, in the midst of the fatigue that had settled upon him since his return home earlier in the afternoon, was that if he did his job well, all of this frantic running around would soon be over.

For now, though, he had another errand to run. Tonight, he would take Mr. Fukushima up to the office where his daughter had been murdered. He was not sure what reaction he should expect. *Best to wait and see,* he thought, as he prepared to head out into the dark streets of the city. He would have to keep a watchful eye on the man, in case he broke down completely, or otherwise became uncontrollable.

Jack had told Rhonda's father that it was to help to bring some closure to the tragedy. *For his sake, and mine, I hope I was telling the truth,* he thought, as he pulled up in front of the office building where the crime had taken place.

Jack's plan was to park here, walk to Fukushima's, and escort Rhonda's father up to Brendan's office. As he passed the door leading to the lobby of the building, he could see

245

that Graham was in his usual place for the evening with his feet on the desk. Jack waved, but the watchman's thoughts were, obviously, elsewhere at the moment.

When Jack came to the little shop, around the corner and down the hill, the proprietor was struggling with the sandwich board.

"Here. Let me help you with that," Jack said, reaching for the wooden sign.

"That is okay. It is not heavy. I'll take it in myself," Mr. Fukushima said, clutching the sign close and hurrying into the shop. After turning off the lights, and arming the security system, he joined Jack on the sidewalk. With a ring of keys in his hand, the man methodically locked the door's deadbolts.

Jack and Mr. Fukushima walked up the hill from the store, without speaking, and stopped at the entrance to the tower that housed the offices of Biggs, Wilberforce, Hutton, and Small, and the place where Rhonda Fukushima took her last breath.

Jack rapped gently on the door, and Graham roused from his reverie. He crossed the concourse, keys in hand, straining to see outside the door, despite the reflections from inside that surely must have been obstructing his view. When he saw Jack, he smiled, and unlocked the door so the two men could enter. Jack made no attempt at introductions.

"We'll just be upstairs for a few minutes. Do I need a key?"

"Yeah, here you go," Graham said, passing a large key ring to Jack. "This one's the key to the office. Lock yourselves in when you get there. I don't expect anyone else will want in, but the place is supposed to be kept secure from intruders, especially since that girl . . ." His voice trailed off as he looked at the man standing with Jack.

"Thanks," Jack said. He and Mr. Fukushima headed for the elevator.

Once aboard, the older man pressed the button for the floor where Brendan's office was located. With no business being transacted in the building at that time of night the trip was a quick one. They stepped out on the eleventh floor.

Jack unlocked the door. Inside the office, a bank of switches controlled the lighting. A few lights were left on, so Graham could look in during his regular circuits through the night. Jack did not know which ones controlled the illumination in the area behind the reception desk so he turned on all of the switches. The whole office was lit up now.

"I'll just lock this door like Graham asked, and then we can go in," Jack said.

He turned to lock the door and gave it a gentle shake, to be sure the bolt had been driven home.

"There. Now we can go back . . ." When he turned around, Gregory Fukushima was not there.

Jack walked past the reception counter, and around the dividing wall, to the main work area. Rhonda's father was standing in the middle of the office, tears in his eyes, looking at the spot where the lifeless body of his daughter had been found. Jack noted that the efficient crew that had followed the police detectives and the IDENT team had erased all traces of the crime.

He stood beside the little man, who looked even smaller as he mourned his daughter's death.

"I'm sorry," was all Jack could manage.

"I'm sorry too," Mr. Fukushima said, wiping his eyes with the back of his hand. "These things should not happen. I am sorry for all the times I was angry with my daughter. Now, it is too late. The past cannot be changed. The future looks very dark."

The grieving father was seized by another wave of sorrow

and cried freely, looking at the place where the blood of his daughter had once stained the carpet. After a few more minutes, he looked at Jack. "We can go now," he said.

The experience had had a profound effect on the man. It had had a different effect on Jack. He escorted his guest to the office door and unlocked it. It took a little experimentation but Jack felt he had made the right selection of light switches to return the area to its previous level of illumination. After re-locking the door, Jack took Mr. Fukushima back to the lobby. He went alone to Graham's desk, where he exchanged the key and a few hushed words. Graham followed the two visitors to the door, locking it after them.

On the sidewalk, Jack asked, "Do you need a ride anywhere?"

"No. I will be fine. My car is just down the hill. Thank you for taking me to the office. I will see you again."

"I'm certain of that, sir." Jack returned the other man's polite bow, and headed to his car.

He watched, as the father of the murdered girl walked slowly around the corner, and disappeared down the hill.

"Well, that was interesting," Jack said to himself, as he pulled away from the curb, and headed back home.

Chapter Thirty-one

Working into the early morning, Jack finished his preparations, overwhelmed by the selfishness and wickedness of his fellow human beings. He was convinced that he was above all that, but then, he reasoned, he had never found himself in a situation that made him feel that desperate.

He finally went to bed, for a fitful night's sleep.

The next morning saw Jack heading through the rush-hour traffic toward police headquarters. In his waking hours, the night before, he had reviewed again and again the details of the past weeks, and had confirmed in his mind that he finally had the information the police needed in order to make an arrest.

He knew the chief detective well enough to believe that he would have a listening audience. Brown was a reasonable man, and one who would wait before passing judgment. If he said Jack's theory was unreasonable, Jack would be willing to accept that evaluation. He didn't believe it would come to that.

The other detective would be a different matter. Keegan Willis was someone you had to convince first. You had to be able to dazzle him with facts and figures, and then eliminate all the other options if the detective felt his theory was the right one.

At the police station, Jack was passed through to the detective division, and went straight to Ted Brown's office. It was empty. He asked about the officer's whereabouts.

"I think he's downstairs with Dr. Walle. We had a homicide last night."

The man, whom Jack did not know, was new to the force. The officer moved on to other work, without pausing to give details. Jack would have to wait a while longer. Willis was also missing. Jack didn't particularly care if Willis didn't show up. It would be one less dissenting voice, he figured.

It was almost three-quarters of an hour before the chief detective returned to his office. Jack had been sitting in a waiting area, reading old magazines. He had seen Brown come back in, and followed him to his work area.

"You got something for me?" the detective asked.

"I think so. In fact I'm pretty certain I've got the solution. It may sound a little wacky, but I've been able to piece things together and I think you should be ready to make an arrest."

"Hold on a second, cowboy, we don't go riding off in all directions just because you think we should. You can get in deep trouble for doing something like that. Before we mount up, you tell me what you've got. I'll let you know when we get to the point of heading out to make an arrest."

Jack did just that for the next hour or so. He reviewed

all the details of the case with the detective, and added the insights he had received from interviews with Rhonda's friends and family, as well as the folks in the office tower.

Willis had joined the debriefing partway through and, as Jack had expected, was less than enthusiastic about the investigator's theory.

Jack pressed on, adding details he had been able to glean from his friend, Ron Leung. It had been Leung, with whom he had spoken a few days earlier, who had sent his thinking in new directions. It was Ron's suggestions that had enabled him to draw the conclusions he was presenting to the detectives.

"I think that if we approach this just the right way, there will be nothing to lose and everything to gain," Jack said.

"How do you figure that?" Willis asked.

The two detectives looked at Jack, with hands on hips, and eyebrows raised.

"I think our suspect will confess, given the proper encouragement. If I'm wrong, nothing will come of it, and everybody's reputation, except mine, is spared for another day. If I'm right, you guys get all the accolades for breaking the case, and my friend Brendan is absolved of all responsibility. What do you say?"

"And you get . . ." Willis let the statement hang in the air.

"I get the satisfaction of being right and, if the truth be known, a nice little reward from Brendan Biggs that should make it all feel worthwhile."

"You better pray you're right about this. You'll be a laughingstock otherwise, and poor to boot." Willis' smirk made Jack ready to fight.

"Well, boys, I think we should stop arguing, and take a little ride," Brown said. "Let's prove Jack right or wrong. I've got nothing else pressing right at this moment. Dr. Walle is going to be tied up with the new homicide for awhile and he'll page me when he's done."

"Time to mount up, Jack," the chief detective added, taking a set of keys from a pegboard behind his desk.

The three men sat in silence as they drove to their destination. Jack was thinking how foolish he would look if his suspicions proved false. He could see, from the smirk on Willis' face, that the detective was hoping for an opportunity to gloat. Brown was keeping his eyes on the road ahead. They finally pulled to a stop and all three got out of the unmarked police car.

Dark brown eyes flickered recognition as Jack walked up. There was no noticeable reaction to the sight of the other two.

"Is he here?" Jack asked.

"Yes, he's back there." A nod of the head indicated direction.

"Maybe you'd better come with us, and hear what I have to say," Jack said. He moved toward the man sitting at the little table. He could hear the sound of shuffling feet, and the heavier footfalls of the two detectives behind him.

"I have some good news and some bad news to share with you both," Jack said.

The Fukushimas looked at Jack with a mixture of sadness and fear.

"Is this about my daughter?" Mrs. Fukushima asked.

"Yes, I'm afraid it is. I'm glad you are still here. I thought you were going away this week," Jack replied.

"My plane leaves this afternoon," the woman said. "What is your news?"

"I think I know who is responsible for your daughter's death. But I think it was an accident. May I ask you both some questions?"

"An accident? How can that be?" the little lady asked.

The two officers were looking on. Brown took a note pad from his pocket, and clicked his ballpoint to readiness.

"What do you want to know?" Gregory Fukushima asked from his little table. He took a sip of his tea.

"I need to tell you, first of all, Mrs. Fukushima, that I am going to have to say some things you are not going to like; some things about your daughter."

The woman stared at the floor, and nodded sadly.

"Mr. Fukushima, you were upset that your daughter was making friends with people who did not appreciate your culture and tradition. You told me that yourself."

The man nodded, and took another sip.

"You felt that Rhonda was bringing disgrace on the Fukushima name. When you heard she was pregnant . . ."

The woman took a deep breath and covered her mouth with her hand.

"When you heard Rhonda was going to have a baby, you were devastated. Then you heard that the father of the child was not Asian, and you became angry. Stop me if I'm getting this wrong."

The man said nothing.

Jack continued. "You decided to confront your daughter, but you did not want your wife to know for fear it would cause her much distress. So you hatched a plan to get your daughter alone, so you could try to convince her to leave James Heddon, and to go away to have the baby in secret."

Mr. Fukushima had put down his cup, and was staring at his hands. He nodded assent.

"You fabricated a story about someone from Biggs, Wilberforce, Hutton, and Small wanting to offer your daughter a full-time job. I'm not sure why you chose the advertising office for your meeting. It had to be a place close to your shop, and it had to be a business that might need a secretary. You gave Rhonda a note you had written. You told your wife that Mr. Biggs had called.

"But, I know that there is no telephone in the store. You don't like using the telephone. You were working that day, so you couldn't possibly have received a message from Biggs.

"When I asked you if it was okay for Rhonda to be out for that interview, you completely evaded the question. But her friends have told me how you always wanted her home by nine every night. I don't believe, after talking to you, that you would have been able to change your mind about Rhonda's curfew that easily."

Fukushima was looking at the three men with apparent emotion now.

Jack continued his commentary. "That afternoon you called the cleaning company, probably from a pay phone, and told them you represented the advertising company. You told them that they would not be needed for the evening. I'm sure it was very difficult for you, considering how you hate to talk on the phone.

"That night you went to the office tower, pretending to be from the cleaning company. You told the guard that you had forgotten your key, and you borrowed his. He was a little hesitant to tell me that, at first.

"I called him, before he left for work yesterday, and asked him to look closely at the man I would be bringing around later that evening. When I returned the key, he told me that he recognized you.

"And then you waited for your daughter to come for her interview. You confronted her with what you knew, and made your proposal. Do I have it right so far?"

Fukushima nodded in the affirmative. His wife stood, shaking, and crying softly.

"I don't think you intended to kill Rhonda. I think you just wanted to make her show you some respect. What happened up there?"

Jack fell silent. The next few moments would either make his case or make him look the fool.

Fukushima looked up with determination in his eyes.

"She laughed at me. She told me I was old fashioned. She said I was living in another age, and that she did not want to be part of it. She told me she was going to marry this Jimmie boy, who had had his way with her. He is not Asian. The baby would not be Asian. I was very angry."

"What did you do, Mr. Fukushima?" Jack asked.

Brown had been writing notes during Jack's interrogation. Willis was standing with his mouth open.

"I did not intend to kill my daughter," the man said. "She had brought dishonor upon my family. She had shown disrespect for me. I had a knife that I carried with me. I used it at the store, and at home. I only wanted to scare her. But she yelled at me, and called me names I had never heard before. I was very angry. I stabbed her once, and then many more times. I could not seem to control myself. I am so sorry, Noriko, I have brought shame upon our household."

"Where is the knife?" Jack asked. "That one you showed me, the other day, can't be the murder weapon."

"I threw it in the garbage. Not the regular garbage—that one," Mr. Fukushima said, pointing to a plastic box under a shelf. "I wasn't sure I wanted to get rid of it, just yet. The one I showed you is a new one. I could not bear to look at the knife that killed my daughter. I tried to clean it but it still has my Ronnie's blood on it. I thought I might be able to use it again, some time, but I can't. I just can't."

The man hung his head and shook it sadly.

Jack turned to the two detectives.

"There is a sign out there on the sidewalk. The morning after the murder, I was driving home. I saw Mr. Fukushima taking it in."

"How is that a clue?" Willis asked, scratching his head.

"It was early morning. He was taking the sign in, not out. I finally figured out that he had left directly from the store, the evening before, and walked around the corner to the office building. But he forgot the sign.

"You took the elevator down to the carpark and went home, didn't you?" Jack said. "You took the knife and tried to clean it. Sometime at night you remembered the sign and had to get it inside. That's why I saw you around six in the morning, the only shopkeeper out at that time of day. That was when you threw the knife away. Well, as it turns out, you didn't entirely get rid of it.

"You told me you were the guilty party when we went up to the office, last night. When we got on the elevator you knew to press the button for the eleventh floor. And then, while I was locking the door behind us, you went to the exact spot where Rhonda had died. You could not have known where that was unless you had been there with her, that night.

"Even before that, you assured me I could tell the police that Brendan Biggs was not responsible for your daughter's death. And, unfortunately, I had been misinterpreting your comments about Jimmie Heddon.

"You kept telling me he was responsible for Rhonda's death. You never said he killed her. You were very careful about that. In your mind, he was responsible for her death because his relationship with your daughter roused your anger, which led to her death."

Willis had gone out and retrieved the sandwich board. Now he rummaged in the box Mr. Fukushima had indicated. Lifting some old newspapers with one hand he reached in.

"It's a switchblade. I've got it," he said. "The lab will be able to find some blood traces by the look of it." He held the weapon up and pressed a button on the handle. A blade snapped to attention.

Jack was relieved to see that Willis had had the presence of mind to put on rubber gloves for this operation.

The detective gently cradled the knife in the palm of his left hand as he shook open an evidence bag with the other. He placed the weapon in the receptacle and sealed it before handing it to his superior.

Mr. Fukushima had a sad, tired countenance. The fight had gone out of him. It was not the fault of the police, or of his wife, or of his dear, dead daughter. He had fought the fight and lost terribly.

Rhonda had become the product of her present environment. It had been no use his harping about the traditions of the homeland that he held so dear. They were his values. She had been swept up in the traditions and practices of her adopted homeland. It was as simple as that.

He had come to North America for its promise of freedom. He had been, and continued to be, free to love his cherished lifestyle, within the laws of his new home. Rhonda had chosen to use that same liberty to live the other lifestyle and, in so doing, had confused her father and angered him by declaring her freedom from his past.

Brown stepped forward now and, taking an elbow, eased Gregory Fukushima to his feet.

"I'm placing you under arrest for the murder of Rhonda Fukushima," Willis intoned. "You have the right to remain silent . . ."

Brown clicked on a pair of handcuffs, placed a hand on the man's back and, using his other hand on a shoulder, guided him out to the street.

Jack caught a glimpse of the tired, sad look, as the man settled himself in the back of the police cruiser.

With a look of terror in her eyes, Mrs. Fukushima watched her husband being led away. Jack did his best to comfort her. She sat at the table, with her face in her hands, and the tears trickled out between her fingers.

"Poor woman," Jack whispered to Willis. "She's just finished burying her daughter. And now her husband is going to prison for Rhonda's murder."

Willis looked genuinely touched by the whole affair. The guy had, at least, some humanity in him, Jack thought.

A patrol car was called to take Mrs. Fukushima back home, after locking up the shop for the rest of the day. Jack rode with her, while Brown and Willis transported Mr. Fukushima to the police station.

Afterwards, the officers drove Jack to police headquarters, where he had left his car.

Now, his emotions were mixed. There was the satisfaction of a job completed. The falsely accused had been vindicated. The real culprit had been found, and would be punished.

As Jack contemplated that, he wasn't sure what sort of punishment Gregory Fukushima should receive. He would be punished for the rest of his life, no matter what sentence the court might pass.

The victim had been well served by the process. But she was dead. Her father was on his way to the certainty of prison, and her mother would be alone in a place she had hoped to share with her husband till her dying day.

Sad, Jack thought, and made up his mind to visit the older woman from time to time.

Mr. Fukushima had almost made it.

Perhaps Jack could help the man's wife make sense of all that had happened. He could show her that her husband had been right about one thing, at least. It was a good place to live. It was a place to live free. She could take the opportunity to enjoy the benefits. One day, hopefully, she would get her husband back.

Later that afternoon, Jack went to the offices of Biggs, Wilberforce, Hutton, and Small, to see Brendan Biggs. He reported to his old friend about the arrest of Rhonda's father.

"I think you can safely assume that the case against you has been dropped," he told Brendan. "The perpetrator has been caught. The story is such a sad one, though. I wish I felt a little more satisfaction."

"Why'd he do it?" Brendan asked.

"My friend, Ron Leung, explained some of it to me. I'm not sure that I understand it all fully. The Asian culture is one that is rich in tradition. The elder Fukushimas brought that age-old culture along with them when they came to this country.

"It worked well in their own age group, but their daughter enjoyed the western culture better. They saw her behavior as disrespect. Her father saw her pregnancy as a blot on the honor of the family. She was seeing a westerner and planned to marry him. To her, it was a natural thing to do, under the circumstances. Dad didn't have that perception. He wanted her out of the way."

"So he killed her," Brendan said.

"No, that was something that happened in the heat of the moment. If he hadn't had the knife he carried for opening his stock, Rhonda might still be alive. Dad had arranged for her to leave town. He'd bought a plane ticket. I suspect when she died, he paid to have the ticket transferred to his wife so she could take Rhonda's remains back to the land of their ancestors. I can't be sure, but I think he might have been planning to turn himself in, after she left. But, we arrived first."

"So what happens now?" Brendan's face showed no sign of happiness.

"Mr. Fukushima will have his day in court, and will probably be found guilty of manslaughter. He'll spend time in prison. His actions will have brought more dishonor on the family name than he might have expected from his daughter's escapades."

"That's really too bad."

Jack couldn't help but agree.

Jack left the office with a handshake and a check that would help to pay all of his overdue bills for some time. Brendan had been very thankful for his reprieve.

Jack only wished he could feel happier with his windfall. He knew there was one person who could cheer him up.

The car door creaked as Jack pulled it open. The window began to fog up almost as soon as he got in and started the engine. He cracked the window open a little and headed home for a shower.

He hoped Valerie would be able to appreciate his company

that evening. The conversation would likely be about this whole business—a debriefing of sorts. Not very romantic, and not what he would have liked, but at least there would be some comfort in the sharing of the pain and frustration.

It was tough work doing what Jack did but he decided that he wouldn't want to do anything else. It was time for someone else to be hunting down the folks who refused to pay their bills. There were people with far greater problems. There were puzzles to be solved. He wanted to help those folks and solve those mysteries.

Valerie was glad to hear from Jack when he called from a pay phone, while his car was being fueled. She was happy to hear that his hunch had worked out. Like the others, she was saddened to hear the circumstances surrounding the death of the young Asian girl. She had heard about the arrest on her police radio. It had also been a topic of intense conversation back at the police station.

"I feel like I could use some company tonight," Jack said. "I know it's a week night, but I don't think I can face my apartment alone. How are you with a debriefing over dinner? I'll bring pizza."

"I'll be home by four," she replied. "How about you plan on showing up sometime after five. I'll break out my best bottle of ginger ale. We can pretend it is Champagne. I'll try to raise your spirits a little, and maybe we can plan our next big night on the town. What do you think?"

Jack agreed that Valerie's plan was a good one, and promised to be at her apartment on time.

The fall air wafted in through the small opening he had left in the window. The car labored up the hill, past the bus terminal. Jack thought, again, about the Fukushimas and their future.

Life will go on, but not quite as planned. Not today, anyway.

He turned toward the bridge, and the road that would lead him home. It was looking, too, as if he was on a new road toward a new future.